NOTICE PERIOD

STORIES WITH A BLEND OF EMOTIONS, EXPECTATIONS, AND UNCERTAINTIES

HEMANT NAG

Author of "Connect with your Boss(es)" & "The Power of Contribution."

INDIA • SINGAPORE • MALAYSIA

ISBN 979-8-89322-681-2

Contents

About the Book

In every professional journey, there are moments of change—entering a new job and eventually moving on. These transitions vary for everyone. Initially, starting a new job brings joy, but as time passes, expectations, emotions, and priorities may shift. Sometimes, uncertainty about the company's commitment or future makes employees feel disconnected, leading them to consider resigning. "Notice Period" tells fictional stories and observations inspired by real experiences. These tales reflect the inner struggles employees face before making the decision to leave and while searching for a new job. Anyone can relate to these stories, whether they are currently working or new to the workforce. The book highlights varied reasons people resign, showing the need for change based on various experiences.

This book will give a message through stories that as time goes on, what employees want from their job can change, influenced by their experiences and what matters most to them. Employees often become attached to their workplace, which makes changes within the company more impactful. Employees may start feeling detached or uncertain about their future, leading them to think about resigning. Making the decision to leave involves a lot of thinking and weighing up the pros and cons.

"Notice Period" tells stories that mirror the thoughts and feelings employees have before they decide to resign. With each turn of the page, readers can see themselves in the characters and relate to their experiences. The book shows several reasons why people decide to leave their jobs, highlighting that change is natural and can be for many distinct reasons. Each character's journey shows the importance of embracing change for personal growth. Whether you are already working or just starting your career, "Notice Period" has something for you.

This book offers a glimpse into the ups and downs of professional life, showing the challenges of making career changes through engaging stories. By sharing relatable experiences, the book helps readers understand that it is okay to seek change and growth in their careers. Whether you are familiar with the workforce or just starting out, the stories in "Notice Period" provide valuable insights into navigating career transitions with confidence and understanding.

Somewhere it is YOU in the characters mentioned in the book.

About the Author

Embarking on a journey that commenced twenty five years ago in the realm of technology, he has navigated through the rich tapestry of the IT industry with unwavering determination and exemplary skill. Starting his career as a technical faculty, he laid the foundational stones of knowledge and expertise, fostering an environment of learning and innovation. This initial role was merely the first chapter in a storied career that saw him evolve through various milestones, from Project Coordinator to the esteemed position of Director of IT Service Delivery, and in present, to Delivery Head.

Throughout his extensive career, the essence of teamwork has been a constant theme. In every role and at every organization, his leadership was characterized by a deep, personal connection with his team. This connection was not just about leading; it was about understanding— the kind of understanding that can only be forged through genuine interaction and shared experiences. By facing and embracing the challenges encountered in professional settings, he had not only led teams but also cultivated communities.

His commitment to enhancing team performance and individual growth extended beyond the conventional boundaries of the workplace. As a Performance Coach, he has conducted multiple workshops both within and outside his organization, imparting wisdom, and techniques to unlock the potential that lies within everyone. His ability to guide, motivate, and inspire has undoubtedly left an indelible mark on countless professionals, empowering them to excel in their roles and personal lives.

Moreover, his ability as a speaker has further amplified his impact on the professional community. With a significant presence on YouTube, he has shared insights on soft skills, a testament to his dedication to nurturing holistic professional development. These videos serve as a beacon for those seeking to enhance their interpersonal skills, communication, and overall professional demeanor, bridging the gap between technical expertise and the soft skills essential for true leadership.

His rich experience, both as a leader and a team member, has culminated in the publication of two notable works: "Connect with Your Boss(es)" and "The Power of Contribution." These books distill his years of experience into accessible wisdom, offering readers strategies for fostering meaningful connections in the workplace and understanding the profound impact of their contributions. Through these writings, he has not only shared his knowledge but also inspired a dialogue on the importance of relationship-building and the value of every individual's work within a larger organizational context.

His career is a testament to the power of connection, leadership, and continuous personal and professional development. His journey from a technical faculty to a Delivery Head of IT services, his role as a Performance Coach, his insights shared through YouTube, and his contributions to the literary world embody a multifaceted approach to professional excellence. As he continues to influence and inspire, his legacy is marked not just by the positions he held, but by the lives he has touched and the positive changes he fostered in the world of professionals.

Introduction

Drawing upon a quarter-century of professional experience, I have come to recognize that the phases of joining and leaving roles are inherent to the rhythm of one's career journey. Throughout my diverse career, I have navigated through the process of resigning and transitioning out of organizations no fewer than ten times. Each departure was prompted by a unique set of needs and aspirations, reflecting the evolving landscape of my professional and personal life.

My career began in the field of technical education, a period marked by frequent transitions between various institutions. This initial stage was largely driven by the pursuit of financial stability and growth. Like many at the outset of their careers, my primary focus was on securing a stronger financial footing, a goal that often necessitated seeking out new opportunities and challenges across different settings.

This journey through multiple educational institutes was not just a quest for better compensation but also an early exploration of the vast possibilities within my profession. It was a time of learning and adaptation, of understanding the nuances of different organizational cultures and educational environments. Each transition, each notice period served, was a stepping-stone that contributed to a broader understanding of my field and my place within it.

Looking back to these experiences underscores the dynamic nature of professional life, where change is the only constant. The decision to leave a position and the subsequent notice period represent critical moments of transition, offering opportunities for reflection, growth, and new beginnings. Whether driven by the need for financial improvement or the quest for broader professional experiences, each move was a chapter in the ongoing narrative of my career, shaping the professional I am today.

When a person decides to resign, going through a notice period is a crucial step to guarantee a smooth handover of responsibilities. This period, however, varies significantly across different organizations. While some may require a notice period of a month, others might extend it to two or even three months. Interestingly, in the United States, the culture of swift transitions is more prevalent, with some individuals able to move on to new opportunities within a mere fifteen days.

Ideally, most people envision a career where they can both contribute to and grow with the same organization over time. The reality, however, often presents various challenges and constraints that may not align with one's professional growth or personal aspirations. Factors such as limited advancement opportunities, desire for a better work-life balance, or the pursuit of a different career path altogether can compel someone to make the difficult decision to leave.

This decision to move on is never made lightly. It involves careful consideration of both the immediate impact and the long-term implications on one's career trajectory. Despite the uncertainties and the emotional toll it may take, the act of resigning and serving a notice period is seen as a necessary transition, one that opens the door to new possibilities and pathways in one's professional journey. It is a testament to the dynamic nature of the workforce, highlighting the constant interplay between individual aspirations and organizational structures.

The act of resigning, of deciding to leave a familiar role for new horizons, is laden with a complex tapestry of emotions and motivations. This book delves into those multifaceted experiences through a collection of real-life narratives, each shedding light on the myriad reasons behind such pivotal decisions. These stories traverse the spectrum of professional life, capturing moments of exhilaration upon receiving a new job offer, only to gradually reveal the undercurrents of dissatisfaction or unfulfillment that can lead one to consider resignation.

Each account serves as a window into the personal journey of an individual—how the initial thrill of acceptance and the promise of a fresh start can sometimes fade into the monotony or misalignment of expectations, driving the desire for change. While financial improvement is frequently cited as a primary motivator for seeking a new position, it is far from the only catalyst. As individuals progress in their careers, gaining knowledge and experience, their goals, needs, and values evolve. The pursuit of professional development, a more meaningful work-life balance, alignment with personal values, or the need for a more supportive and stimulating work environment are just as compelling.

These narratives reveal that the decision to resign is rarely straightforward or solely financially driven. It is often the culmination of a deep introspection about one's career path, aspirations, and the quest for a role that not only rewards but also challenges and fulfills. This book aims to explore these diverse stories, offering readers a nuanced understanding of the professional landscape and the personal growth that accompanies each transition. Through these real-time stories, readers will discover the multifaceted reasons that compel individuals to embark on new paths and the rich, sometimes unexpected, emotional journeys that unfold as a result.

Throughout my career, I too have been on the receiving end of numerous resignation letters, each telling its own unique story. These experiences have afforded me a comprehensive view of the myriad reasons that compel individuals to make the significant decision to resign and navigate the complexities of serving their notice period.

The motivations behind these resignations are as diverse as the individuals themselves. Often, the reasons are rooted in genuine necessity—personal circumstances, family commitments, health issues, or the pursuit of opportunities that align more closely with their long-term career goals or values. These are moments of transition, driven by a clear-eyed assessment of what is needed for their growth or well-being.

Conversely, there are instances where the drive to resign stems from an abundance of ambition. In these cases, the desire for rapid advancement, higher compensation, or more prestigious roles can fuel a restless aspiration that outpaces the opportunities available within the current role or organization. This ambition, while commendable for its forward-looking nature, sometimes leads to decisions based on the lure of potential rather than the reality of the present.

Both scenarios reflect the complex interplay of personal and professional aspirations that define our working lives. Witnessing these resignations unfold has provided me with invaluable insights into the human aspects of career progression, the varied paths we choose, and the multitude of factors that influence these pivotal decisions. It is a reminder of the personal journeys that underpin each resignation letter, each notice period served—a narrative of change, aspiration, and the search for fulfillment.

This book is an invitation to explore these stories, offering insights into the myriad reasons behind career transitions, and perhaps, encouraging you to reflect on your own professional journey and the possibilities that lie ahead.

In my tenure, the narratives I bring to you are reflections of the genuine scenarios I have witnessed firsthand. On numerous occasions, a lack of clear communication and adequate explanations to team members has led to unintended consequences. This absence of transparency and understanding has, regrettably, driven individuals to feel disconnected and undervalued, compelling them to sever their ties with the organization. These instances are not mere anecdotes but rather poignant illustrations of the critical importance of open dialogue and meaningful engagement within the workplace. They underscore the profound impact that effective communication can have on team cohesion, morale, and ultimately, on the decision of talented individuals to stay with or leave an organization.

Prologue

There are many stories out there where for several reasons, what started as a smooth journey at a job ends up in leaving the company. Nowadays, it is rare to find someone who stays in one job all the way until retirement. It used to be common, like with our parents or grandparents, who often started and ended their careers in the same place. They would stick it out, no matter the situation. But today, things have changed. With so many different job options available in all sorts of fields, everyone has the chance to move on if they want to. This makes it easier for people to seek happiness, meet their needs, and achieve their dreams by exploring new opportunities.

Individuals who decide to leave their current employment and seek new opportunities for reasons like insufficient pay, limited prospects for advancement, uninspiring leadership, a lack of purposeful work, unsupportive team members, and insufficient flexibility in the workplace, feel disrespected among others. Additionally, the propensity to switch jobs differs significantly between those at the beginning of their careers and seasoned professionals.

Over time, individuals increasingly align their employment choices with their professional objectives. Early in their careers, people today are more inclined to switch jobs for relatively minor reasons, but this tendency diminishes with experience. This is because, at entry level, opportunities to move are plentiful, reflecting the wider availability of positions that require less specific expertise. In contrast, as one ascends the career ladder, opportunities become scarcer, necessitating a closer match between an individual's skills and the demands of higher-level roles. This evolution illustrates a natural maturation in career trajectories, where both priorities and opportunities shift in tandem with personal growth and professional development.

The reasons people want to change jobs can be different depending on how much they earn. People with higher incomes might look for jobs that make them happier or pay even better, while those with lower incomes often want a job that offers more money or job security. However, not everyone feels they can make a change.

Embarking on a journey with a new organization is often pursued with optimism, a search for fulfillment, and a yearning for a happier phase in one's career. However, there comes a pivotal moment, a trigger, that sometimes shifts the narrative, leading to a parting of ways. This juncture marks the beginning of new tales, woven with a rich tapestry of emotions, desires, and anticipations.   This book invites readers to traverse through an array of such stories, each chronicling the diverse experiences of joy, aspirations, and the inevitable challenges that professionals face in the modern workplace.

Recruiting a new member into an organization is a complex, resource-intensive endeavor, encompassing a myriad of strategic decisions and investments in time and capital. Conversely, the decision to depart, though deeply personal and often difficult, is made by the individual, standing in simple contrast to the collective efforts invested in their recruitment and integration. This separation highlights the intricate dynamics of workplace relationships and the profound impact of individual choices on the collective fabric of an organization.

As you delve into the pages of this book, you will encounter a variety of narratives that capture the essence of professional life, offering insights into the multifaceted nature of employment, the pursuit of career advancement, and the quest for personal fulfillment within the workplace. These stories transcend mere stories; they serve as reflections on the shared human experience, providing valuable lessons on resilience, adaptability, and the pursuit of happiness in one's career.

This book is not confined to any specific age group or demographic; it resonates with the universal experiences of individuals navigating the complexities of the modern job market. Whether you are at the onset of your career, contemplating a notable change, or reflecting on the path you have traversed, these stories offer a mirror to your own journey, inviting introspection, understanding, and, ultimately, growth.

This collection of tales is a celebration of the human spirit, its capacity to adapt, to overcome, and to find meaning in the medley of professional life. It is an invitation to explore the depth of our aspirations, to embrace the uncertainties of change, and to discover the boundless potential within each of us to craft a fulfilling career. Embark on this journey with an open heart and a curious mind, and may you find within these pages both reflection and inspiration, guiding you towards your own path of fulfillment and success in the ever-evolving landscape of work.

CHAPTER 1

The Launchpad

"There's always anxiety when you start a new job, you are the one guy who doesn't know where the ketchup is"

– Jon Stewart

Anne received her first offer letter to work as a junior designer in one of the companies in Jaipur. It was her day to celebrate. Her doors were opened for her career. She started dreaming about her professional journey and preferably in the same organization. Of course, she had a good reason to feel this way. She had finished her internship there, and over the last six months, she learned a lot more through her work experience than she ever did in her regular college classes.

She started college with the hope of getting a good internship and finally a job. Every year she used to listen to her teachers or placement cell about how many students had been absorbed, on what package it was, in which city etc. That always excited her about the job. She selected her favorite subject to do specialization and worked closely on how to crack interviews, aptitude tests, communication, and other soft skills. It was not an easy journey for her to pass through any company selection process where all her colleagues and friends were also fighting for that.

Out of nowhere, her friend and now colleague, Raman, excitedly interrupted her thoughts. "Hey Anne, congratulations on becoming an employee! Our intern days are behind us. We are officially starting our careers and getting our salaries this month. Come on, let us go to thank our mentor, Priya, together." Anne agreed and with Raman and a few other freshly appointed team members they went to meet their manager. As they moved across the office floor, the youthful energy huddled together in groups, playfully pushing, and occasionally whispering among themselves, as if they were trying to blend into the background. The friendly and slightly nervous behavior of the new, young employees caught the attention of others in the office. Seeing how charming and inexperienced they were, the other employees could not help but smile. Their hesitation was real, a mix of excitement and nervousness, as they navigated through the workspace. Their sole focus was on reaching their mentor's desk, all the while doing their best to avoid drawing too much attention or making direct eye contact with the more seasoned staff members around them. This cautious approach highlighted their transition from the academic world into the professional realm, carrying with them an air of eager anticipation mixed with a hint of uncertainty. As soon as they reached Priya's table in the group, she took no time to understand the reason for coming. She was observing happiness on their faces, they were excited, and it seemed that they could do any miracle in life. Anne greeted her and conveyed her thanks to Priya. At the same time all the others also conveyed their gratitude to Priya. Priya was incredibly happy listening to them and took all of them into the conference room.

Gathering the newly confirmed employees around her, Priya posed a question that resonated deeply, "How do you feel now, holding your confirmation letters?" Their responses were not spoken, but clearly visible in the brightness of their smiles and the eager anticipation in their eyes. It was a moment of shared achievement and optimism. With genuine warmth, Priya extended her congratulations to the group, her voice carrying both pride and encouragement. "Your journey to this point has been about proving your worth, about demonstrating that you have what it takes to be part of this organization. You have succeeded in that challenge. But the journey doesn't end here; it evolves. Now, you're tasked with contributing to our collective growth, bringing your unique skills and perspectives to the forefront."

Then, Priya began to share snippets of her own professional journey, providing a personal narrative that bridged her initial steps as a newcomer to her current role. She spoke of the challenges she faced, the milestones she celebrated, and the relentless pursuit of growth that propelled her forward. Her story was not just a recounting of her past but a testament to the potential that lay within each of them to shape their paths and contribute to the organization.

Reflecting on her own contributions, Priya felt a deep sense of pride. She had played a pivotal role in assembling this vibrant team of skilled individuals including Anne, Raman, and others, each selected for their potential to bring fresh energy and innovative ideas to the company. As she looked at the faces before her, Priya was reminded of the impact one person could make, not just in their own career but in nurturing the next generation of talent. This moment was more than a milestone for the new employees; it was a celebration of a cycle of growth and mentorship that continued to drive the organization forward.

Filled with a sense of achievement and excitement, Anne, Raman, and the rest of the newly appointed team members could not wait to share the news of their significant milestone with their families. The moment they announced their successful employment, their homes buzzed with an overwhelming sense of joy and pride. Family members, brimming with excitement, quickly began showering them with blessings and words of encouragement, recognizing the beginning of a new chapter in their lives. It was a momentous occasion, marking their transition from students to professionals, a step into a new era filled with possibilities and challenges. The warmth and support from their loved ones underscored the significance of this achievement, not just as a personal victory but as a collective one, celebrating the promise of a bright and promising future ahead.

For Anne, getting this job meant more than just having work; it was a big sign of how much her family had given up and hoped for her success. She was acutely aware of the lengths her parents went to ensure her education, from mortgaging her mother's precious ornaments to her father's relentless efforts as a ward boy in a private hospital. Her mother, too, contributed to cleaning homes to add to the family's meager income. Even though they worked extremely hard, Anne's family did not earn enough money for their needs in today's expensive world, so Anne had to go to a government school.

Yet, Anne's world was one of vibrant colors and intricate designs, her passion for art evident in every piece she created. Recognizing her talent and determination, her parents stretched their finances to the limit to afford her a place in a reputable design college—a decision far beyond their financial reach but fueled by hope and ambition. They did all this with a single goal in mind: to see Anne thrive in a rewarding corporate role, where her skills could shine, and her contributions valued. This job was more than a career start; it was the fulfillment of her family's shared sacrifices and dreams, a beacon of hope for a brighter and more secure future.

Overwhelmed by these reflections, a wave of emotion swept over Anne, bringing tears to her eyes. As she gently wiped away the moisture that blurred her vision a strong determination grew inside her. With a heart full of gratitude for her family's sacrifices and a mind set on her future, she made a solemn promise to herself. Anne was determined not just to work alongside her seniors but to truly excel, to become an indispensable asset to her team. This commitment was not merely about fulfilling her professional duties; it was about honoring her parents' hard work and dreams. Anne was ready to channel all her talent, passion, and the values instilled by her upbringing into making a significant impact, proving through her actions that their faith in her was well placed.

As time unfurled, the days and months seamlessly blended into a journey of growth and learning. Anne and her colleagues, each fueled by the strength of their first professional endeavor, threw themselves into their work with unparalleled dedication. Immersed in live projects that tested their limits and expanded their horizons, they were steadfast in their commitment to excel. This initial phase of their careers found them perpetually eager, always on the brink of discovery, ready to leap at any opportunity to prove their mettle. Their ethos was one of relentless optimism and resilience; the word 'no' was absent from their vocabulary. Weekdays melded into weekends as they willingly devoted extra hours, driven by a shared ambition to stand out, to be recognized not merely as competent but as exemplary in their roles. This period was marked by a collective zeal to contribute, to learn, and to affirm their value within the organization.

Within the landscape of mid-sized organizations, the starting salary often reflects the geographical and economic disparities between cities categorized into Tiers A, B, and C, as well as depending on the organization's size and industry sector. Anne found herself at the heart of this reality, embarking on her career journey with a modest organization nestled in a Tier B city. The compensation offered to her, while humble, was the cornerstone of her professional beginnings—an opportunity that marked her entry into the workforce, her very first step on the corporate ladder.

This initial salary, though nominal, was a symbol of Anne's transition from academic pursuits to real-world challenges. It represented her first foray into financial independence, a critical milestone despite its modesty. However, as the year unfolded, so did Anne's aspirations and her dedication to her role. Her involvement in projects, her commitment to excellence, and her growing skill set fueled a desire for more—a longing not just for personal advancement, but for the ability to provide a more comfortable life for her family.

Anne held onto the hope for a significant leap forward, envisioning a future where her contributions would not only be recognized but rewarded in a manner that reflected her value to the organization. She dreamed of a day when her salary would not just cover the basics but offer her and her family a sense of security and comfort, a testament to her hard work and the sacrifices that paved the way for her career. This yearning for growth, for a transition that would bring her professional satisfaction and the means to uplift her loved ones, became a driving force in Anne's journey, pushing her to strive for excellence in every task she undertook.

The day finally arrived for Anne and her colleagues to fill out their very first appraisal forms—a big deal for anyone new to the working world. This was their chance to talk about what they had done over the year and hopefully get a nice bump in their salary. Understandably, they were all pretty focused on how much of a raise they might get since it was their first time through this process.

Anne was no different. She wanted to make sure she did everything right to get a good raise. So, she went over to her friend Raman to ask for some advice. They were both new to this and had lots of questions about how to fill out the forms correctly. It was all new and a bit confusing. Soon, their whole group got together to figure it out. They spent a lot of time talking about what to write down. They wanted to make sure they said plenty of good things about their work, their seniors, and the company. They thought it was important to show they were positive about their jobs and to talk up the good parts of working there.

It was a team effort to help each other, with everyone chipping in with ideas on how to make their forms look as good as possible. They all wanted to impress and show they were valuable to the company, hoping it would lead to a nice raise. It was a mix of wanting to do well for themselves and wanting to fit in well with what the company was looking for. When the moment arrived, Anne, Raman and all others received an email of their very first increment letter in their inbox. It is as if time itself pauses, allowing them to savor the weight of this milestone. The pdf file on official letterhead, becomes tangible evidence to their journey of growth, effort, and perseverance. It's more than just a letter; it's a symbol of recognition, an encouragement of promising professional identity.

When Anne clicked to open her increment letter on the computer, she was flooded with so many feelings. The amount of the raise was much lower than she had hoped for, leaving her in disbelief. "Is this really happening?" she thought, feeling let down. It seemed like all the challenging work she had put in had not been noticed at all. For a moment, she was completely shocked, struggling to understand why the reward for her hard work was so small.

She looked around at her friends, trying to figure out if they felt the same way. Anne was not sure if she should talk to someone about her disappointment or just keep quiet. While some of her teammates seemed okay with their raises, Anne felt as if her dreams and expectations had been dashed. She was filled with questions. "Do I have to wait a whole other year for a better raise?"

This question weighed heavily on her, making her wonder whether she should stick it out and hope for more next year or start thinking about finding a job that might value her efforts more.

Anne spent the entire night wrestling with her feelings of disappointment, her mind a tumult of frustration and disbelief. The following day, she mustered the courage to approach her manager,

Jasmeet, seeking clarity and a glimmer of hope. She cautiously broached the subject of her increment, expressing how the actual outcome had fallen short of her expectations, especially considering the effort and dedication she had poured into her work.

Managers like Jasmeet are often well-prepared for these conversations, having been briefed on the rationale behind the team's increments and trained in addressing common concerns by senior management. Jasmeet, therefore, responded to Anne's queries with a rehearsed explanation, delivering the company's stance on the matter without deviation. This response, though expected, felt to Anne like a rehearsed script, lacking the personal acknowledgment she had hoped for.

In that moment of candid exchange, Anne began to see the bigger picture. She recognized that her professional journey was still in its infancy, with only a year of contribution behind her but a vast expanse of potential ahead. This realization sparked a shift in her mindset; she understood that while the immediate reward might not have matched her expectations, the path to recognition and success was a long one, requiring patience, resilience, and continuous effort.

With a renewed sense of purpose, Anne decided to channel her initial disappointment into motivation. She convinced herself to view the situation not as a setback, but as a stepping-stone, an early challenge in her career marathon. Energized by this perspective, she committed to redoubling her efforts, setting her sights on the next year as an opportunity to prove her value and achieve the recognition she aspired to. This decision marked a pivotal moment in Anne's journey, reigniting her determination to pursue her professional goals with even greater zeal.

Jasmeet felt a deep sense of pride inside. He had just managed to carefully guide a difficult conversation with Anne, who was feeling unhappy, to a successful conclusion. He skillfully addressed her concerns and helped her understand the situation better, which was not an easy task. He understood that part of his role was to address and alleviate such concerns, and in this instance, he felt he had managed to do just that. The reality is individuals in the initial stages of their careers often wrestle with the complexities surrounding increments, budgets, and salary structures. For many, the transition from academic achievements to professional rewards can be shaking. They equate challenging work directly with substantial rewards, much like the clear correlation between effort and grades seen in their academic lives.

This gap in understanding underscores the importance of the Human Resources team, supervisors, and mentors in providing guidance and education to these early-career professionals. Jasmeet recognized that it was crucial to offer insight into how the increment process works, the constraints of budgeting, and the rationale behind salary bands. Such conversations are essential not only for setting realistic expectations but also for helping newcomers navigate their initial years in the workforce with a better grasp of their growth path.

Educating young professionals about these processes and planning frameworks is more than about managing expectations; it is about empowering them with knowledge. This understanding enables them to align their personal aspirations with the realistic growth opportunities available within the organization. Jasmeet's interaction with Anne wasn't just about addressing her immediate concerns; it was a step towards fostering a deeper understanding of how career progression and financial rewards intersect, laying the groundwork for a more informed and mutually beneficial relationship between employees and the organization.

Key observations from the chapter –

Onboarding and Initial Experiences: The excitement and enthusiasm of new employees, as depicted by Anne and her colleagues, underscore the importance of a positive onboarding experience. Organizations should ensure that new hires feel welcomed, valued, and integrated into the company culture from day one. This sets the tone for their entire career journey within the company.

Mentorship and Guidance: Priya's role as a mentor to Anne and her colleagues highlights the critical importance of mentorship in the workplace. Organizations should foster an environment where experienced professionals are encouraged to share their journeys, challenges, and insights. This not only inspires new employees but also strengthens the organization's culture of continuous learning and growth.

Recognition and Feedback: The anticipation and response to the first increment letter demonstrates the significant impact of recognition and feedback on employee motivation and satisfaction. Organizations should develop transparent, fair, and regular feedback mechanisms that acknowledge employees' efforts and contributions, guiding them towards their professional goals.

Communication on Compensation: Anne's disappointment with her increment and the subsequent conversation with Jasmeet reveal a gap in communication regarding compensation policies. Organizations need to be transparent about how increments are determined, including the factors considered and the budget constraints. Clear communication can manage expectations and reduce dissatisfaction.

Professional Development Opportunities: Anne's journey from an intern to a junior designer, and her aspirations for growth, underscore the need for organizations to provide clear pathways for professional development. Investing in training programs, skill enhancement workshops, and career progression plans can help retain talent and align employee aspirations with organizational goals.

Support System and Work Environment: The narrative also stresses the importance of a supportive work environment where employees, especially those at the beginning of their careers, feel comfortable seeking advice and expressing their concerns. Creating a culture that encourages open dialogue between employees and management can foster a sense of belonging and improve job satisfaction.

Understanding Individual Aspirations: The varied reactions of Anne and her colleagues to their increments suggest that employees have individual aspirations and circumstances influencing their expectations from the job. Organizations should strive to understand these personal goals and work towards aligning them with the company's objectives.

Holistic Approach to Employee Well-being: Anne's backstory, including her family's sacrifices for her education, highlights the broader context of employees' lives outside work. Organizations should adopt a holistic approach to employee well-being, recognizing and supporting the diverse backgrounds and challenges their employees face.

Fostering a Culture of Appreciation: The collective effort of Anne and her colleagues to impress and show their value to the company, especially during appraisal time, points to the need for a culture that continuously appreciates and rewards hard work and innovation beyond the annual appraisal cycle.

Managing Career Expectations: Finally, Jasmeet's handling of Anne's concerns after her first increment reflects the delicate balance supervisors must maintain in managing career expectations. Providing constructive feedback, setting realistic goals, and offering clear guidance on achieving career aspirations are essential components of effective leadership within an organization.

CHAPTER 2

Coffee Table

"You never change things by fighting the existing reality. To change something, build a new model that makes the existing model obsolete".

— R. Buckminster Fuller

Fueled by a renewed sense of optimism, Anne dedicated herself to her current project, holding onto the belief that this year, her efforts would truly shine. She reflected on how effectively Jasmeet had dispelled her doubts, skillfully easing the burden of stress that weighed on her. Although her financial situation remained a concern, Anne recognized this as a reality of the professional environment she was part of. Determined to overcome the emotional turmoil stirred by the disappointing news in her increment letter, she focused on regaining her mental equilibrium. Anne understood that the path to recovery lay in immersing herself in her work and seeking solace and distraction through casual conversations with her colleagues. This approach, she believed, was crucial in moving forward and regaining her confidence and focus.

With this perspective, Anne reached out to Raman, her closest friend since their college days, suggesting they head to the cafeteria for a tea break. The two made their way to the canteen and placed an order for two cups of coffee. While waiting for their coffee, Raman cast a concerned glance towards Anne. Breaking the silence, he gently broached the subject that had been on his mind. "Anne, since yesterday, it's been clear from your expression that the increment this time hasn't set well with you," he began, his voice filled with empathy. He continued, "I get why a significant raise is so important for you right now." His words, thoughtful and perceptive, acknowledged the gravity of Anne's situation. Raman's keen observation and understanding highlighted the depth of their friendship, showing he not only noticed her distress but also grasped the underlying reasons why financial recognition was critical for Anne at this juncture in her career.

Anne responded with a tone of acceptance, acknowledging the reality of their professional landscape. "It's just how things are, and we need to come to terms with it," she reflected. Sharing insights from her conversation with Jasmeet, Anne mentioned that the discussion had shed light on the intricacies of the appraisal process. "Right now, I might not hold much leverage, but I am optimistic. I believe that as I continue to gain experience and consistently deliver strong results, my contributions will be recognized more significantly. I am confident that this will lead to a much more substantial increment in the future," she expressed with conviction. Her words conveyed a sense of hope and determination, illustrating her readiness to face the challenges ahead with resilience and a belief in her own potential for growth.

As Anne took a thoughtful sip of her coffee, a sudden insight dawned on her. Engrossed in the turmoil of her own grievances and the maze of challenges she faced; she had inadvertently neglected to consider Raman's situation regarding his increment. In a swift motion, she raised her gaze to meet Raman's, her eyes reflecting a mix of embarrassment and concern.

With a sincere tone, she quickly apologized, "Oh, Raman, I am truly sorry. I have been so wrapped up in my own feelings about the increment that it completely slipped my mind to ask about yours.

How did your review go? I am guessing your experience might have been quite like mine, right?" Her words, laden with empathy and a genuine sense of regret for the oversight, highlighted not only her self-awareness but also her deep care for Raman's well-being, shining a light on the strength and compassion that characterized their friendship. Anne had naturally assumed that Raman would receive an increment similar to hers, believing that company policies would uniformly apply to everyone in the same manner. Therefore, it came as a significant shock to her when she discovered that Raman had received an 8% higher hike than she had. This revelation jolted her, unsettling her more than she anticipated. As she took the next sip of her coffee, the bitterness seemed to intensify, not just from the brew itself but from the sting of realizing the disparity in their increments. This newfound knowledge added a layer of complexity to her feelings, making the coffee taste more bitter with each sip as she grappled with the implications of this unexpected difference. Raman's intention was never to boast or imply that he was in any way superior to Anne. When she inquired about his increment, he simply shared the details with the honesty and openness characteristic of their friendship. His response was driven by transparency and the mutual trust that defined their relationship, not by any desire to flaunt his success. He understood the sensitivity of the topic and aimed to communicate his news in a manner that was forthright yet considerate of Anne's feelings.

However, it is natural for people to sometimes fall into the trap of negative thoughts, especially when comparisons come into play. In this situation, Anne found herself grappling with these very emotions. The act of comparing her increment with Raman's inadvertently stirred a sense of unease within her, highlighting how easily one can be swept up by feelings of inadequacy or unfairness. This is a common human experience, where the tendency to measure our own achievements against those of others can lead to discomfort and self-doubt. Caught in a whirlwind of emotions, Anne found herself at a crossroads, unsure whether to celebrate Raman's higher increment with genuine happiness or to voice her frustration over the perceived inequality demonstrated by their organization. With a forced smile that barely concealed her inner turmoil, she offered Raman her congratulations. However, her facial expressions betrayed her true feelings, making it evident that she was struggling with the news. Raman, perceptive and empathetic, quickly noticed Anne's discomfort. Understanding her dilemma, he gently attempted to address her concerns, hoping to soothe the storm of negative emotions brewing within her. He spoke with care, aiming to provide a perspective that might help Anne reconcile her feelings and find peace with the situation, all while navigating the delicate balance between sharing in his good news and acknowledging the disparity between their skill set.

Raman endeavored to gently illuminate the situation for Anne, suggesting that his slightly higher increment could be attributed to the distinct skill set he has been honing and applying in their projects. He explained that in the professional realm, salary bands often reflect the diversity of skills across distinct roles, especially when those skills are aligned with the company's strategic needs. "Even though our experiences are parallel, as we navigate the complexities of the real world, the specific skills we bring to the table become increasingly pivotal," he shared thoughtfully.

He continued, offering an insight into the nuanced dynamics of organizational valuation of skills. "I've come to understand, through countless conversations and observations, that while every skill is valuable, some are considered niche or in higher demand based on current business priorities. It's not a reflection of the importance of one's work but rather an alignment with what drives the core business forward at this moment."

Raman wanted to ensure Anne knew this was not about the quantity of effort or the dedication one shows. "From what I have seen, you're not just working hard; you are often going above and beyond what I do. However, in the corporate world, the economic value assigned to our roles and skills can vary significantly. This does not diminish your contributions in any way. It's just a matter of how these contributions are quantified against the backdrop of business objectives."

His words were meant to offer a broader perspective on how organizations assess and reward different skills, hoping to mitigate her feelings of unfairness. Raman aimed to educate Anne on this aspect of professional life, emphasizing the complex interplay between skill sets, market demand, and business strategy in determining compensation, all while affirming the value of her hard work and dedication.

The deep connection between Anne and Raman played a pivotal role in her receptiveness to his perspective. She grasped the essence of his explanations, which sparked curiosity within her. "How did you come to understand all these nuances?" she inquired, genuinely intrigued by the breadth of his insight. Raman shared that his understanding stemmed from conversations with friends employed across various organizations. These discussions had opened his eyes to the universal nature of increment processes and the factors influencing them. He elaborated, "It's through these exchanges that I've learned about the commonality of experiences when it comes to increments. Each story echoed a similar theme—the value an individual contributes to an organization is often measured against the backdrop of current market demands and the unique skills they possess." Raman's informal research through dialogues with peers had equipped him with a broader understanding of how businesses assess the worth of their employees' contributions. This insight helped Anne see beyond the confines of their own organization, recognizing the intricate balance between personal achievement and the strategic needs that drive recognition and reward in the professional landscape.

Now, the situation had become crystal clear to Anne: merely hoping for a higher increment was futile. She understood that proactive efforts and a commitment to ongoing learning are crucial for achieving growth within any organization. However, this realization brought with it a pressing concern—she worried that if she persisted with her existing skill set, she might find herself in the same disappointing situation when the next appraisal came around. The question that loomed large in her mind was what additional skills she needed to acquire to avoid facing such a setback again due to the absence of specialized expertise. Anne pondered deeply about the future, contemplating the diverse skill sets that could elevate her value to the organization and ensure her contributions were not only recognized but also rewarded in alignment with her aspirations and the company's evolving needs. This moment of introspection marked a turning point, prompting her to consider a strategic approach towards her professional development and career route.

For Anne, financial growth was not just a measure of success; it was a vital means to transform her life and the lives of her loved ones. With improved financial stability, she envisioned overcoming the myriad challenges her family faced. She saw the possibility of supporting her parents more significantly, fulfilling shared dreams of outings and experiences that had, until now, seemed out of reach. Recognizing that achieving such financial security required rapid professional advancement, Anne concluded that she needed to pivot her skill set towards a more in-demand technology.

Determined, Anne began to seek out information on the leading technologies that could enhance her career prospects. She consulted with her seniors and managers, valuing their insights and guidance on making a strategic decision. Based on her strengths and interests, she was directed towards a particular niche area that was experiencing growth and demand in the industry.

However, transitioning to this new field meant that Anne had to dedicate her personal time to learning and mastering this specialty, as her current expertise was in design. This not only required her to manage her time efficiently but also to immerse herself in a completely new domain. Additionally, to formally validate her proficiency and commitment to this new direction, Anne understood she would need to undergo rigorous examination to earn a certification. This path she was about to embark on was not just about acquiring new knowledge; it was a test of her dedication, her ability to balance her existing responsibilities with her aspirations, and her commitment to securing a better future for herself and her family.

Anne faced a new self-set challenge, learning cutting-edge technology while keeping up with her regular project work. Luckily, she was not alone on this journey. Many of her colleagues were more than willing to help her understand the basics and clear up any confusion she had. But to really get good at this new tech, Anne knew she had to put in extra time and effort, more than her usual work required.

Every time she sat down to learn, she thought about how this could lead to better pay and a more comfortable life for her and her family. This thought kept her going, even when the learning got tough. Since this technology was completely new to her, it took a lot of time to understand. On top of that, Anne had to make sure she did not fall behind in her regular job, which paid her bills and was crucial for her daily life.

So, Anne was juggling her current job and her new learning goal. It was a tough balance, showing how determined she was to grow in her career and improve her financial situation for her family's future.

Over the course of six to seven months, Anne devoted her extra hours diligently acquiring new skills, a testament to her commitment and perseverance. This period of intense learning was driven by a clear goal: to achieve certification in her chosen technology. When the moment arrived to take the certification exam, Anne approached it with a blend of nerves and confidence, the culmination of her hard work and dedication. The effort paid off—she passed the exam, a significant milestone on her professional journey.

The joy Anne experienced upon seeing her passing results was immeasurable. This certification was not just a piece of paper; it was a key that unlocked new doors in her career, offering her the opportunity to chart a different path. It validated her skills and hard work, placing her among a select group of professionals with specialized expertise.

With the certificate in hand, Anne began to envision a future where she stood shoulder to shoulder with experts in her field. She saw herself as part of an elite group, contributing valuable insights and leading projects with her newly acquired knowledge. This vision of her future was not just a dream but a tangible possibility, fueled by her newfound certification. It marked a turning point in her career, promising a journey filled with growth, challenges, and the chance to make a significant impact in her niche area.

As Anne approached the completion of another year at her company, she found herself on the tip of a potentially transformative moment in her career. With the annual appraisal on the horizon, she was optimistic for a substantial increment. This optimism was supported by the valuable lessons and knowledge she had gained over time through her continuous effort and dedication. Indeed, life seemed poised to turn a new page in Anne's journey, one filled with promising developments and opportunities.

This period of anticipation was markedly different from the previous year. Anne's confidence was at an all-time high, fortified by her expanded expertise. No longer just a designer, she successfully acquired a set of niche skills that were highly sought after in the market. This unique combination of abilities set her apart, making her a more valuable asset to her organization.

With two years of experience under her belt, Anne had moved beyond the ranks of the newest employees. She was now a bit more seasoned, a professional who not only had time on her side but also a diversified skill set that spanned both creative design and specialized technical knowledge.

This newfound confidence was palpable as she prepared her appraisal form, reflecting on a year that had not only seen her grow in capability but also in recognition. Her achievements over the year, including receiving client appreciation, were testament to her contributions and the positive impact she had made. This was a defining moment for Anne. The combination of her dual skill set, her growing experience, and the acknowledgment of her hard work through awards set the stage for what she hoped would be a significant leap forward in her career trajectory.

For any team looking to grow and succeed, keeping talented members like Anne is often a priority for senior staff. They know that dedicated team members contribute to better project outcomes, which in turn, can lead to happier clients. This year, Anne was eager to highlight the extra knowledge and hard work she had put in over the past year. However, the way Anne saw her contributions was quite different from her manager's perspective.

Jasmeet, Anne's manager, was aware of Anne's dedication. He understood that Anne had been unbelievably valuable to their project and consistently achieving what was required of her and often doing even better than what was expected. Jasmeet was fully aware of Anne's contributions and performance, acknowledging her as a key member of the team whose efforts had positively impacted the project's success. She had shown a remarkable willingness to step out of her comfort zone by picking up new skills. From Jasmeet's standpoint, there was no reason to give Anne a low rating. However, the decision on financial rewards, such as salary increases, does not solely rest with managers like Jasmeet. Those decisions are typically made by higher-ups in the company, based on the budget available for raises. So, while Jasmeet's feedback on Anne's performance was crucial and could influence her appraisal positively, he did not have the power to decide the financial aspect of her rise. This situation highlights the complexity of the appraisal process, where a manager's support is vital, but the final financial decision lies elsewhere.

Jasmeet understood that when it came time to allocate the budget for raises, Anne might not receive the amount she hoped for. He was familiar with Anne's financial situation and knew that she was seeking a better salary not for luxury, but to support her family's needs. Recognizing the importance of this, Jasmeet even brought up Anne's circumstances with the department head Raghu, hoping to make a case for her.

When the day finally arrived for salary updates, everyone was eager to see their new figures. Anne did receive an increase, but it fell short of her expectations. Feeling let down, she did not hesitate to express her disappointment. She quickly drafted a note to Jasmeet and the HR department, voicing her dissatisfaction. In her message, Anne outlined all her contributions and questioned why the company was unable to meet her salary expectations. Her intent was clear: she wanted an explanation for the discrepancy between her performance and the financial recognition she received.

Jasmeet, known for his practical and thoughtful management style, was not surprised by Anne's email. Concerned about its impact on the project, he sought out Raghu for a discussion. Jasmeet praised Anne's rapid adaptation to new skills despite her relatively short two-year tenure, emphasizing how invaluable she was to the team.

Raghu, in response, was sympathetic. He reassured Jasmeet that he had done everything possible to secure Anne a significant increment within the constraints of their budget. He explained that Anne's raise was comparatively generous, designed to reflect her current level of experience and potential for growth. Raghu suggested that it might be helpful to clarify to Anne that her increase was part of a regular appraisal process, distinct from a salary negotiation or major revision.

Furthermore, Raghu highlighted Anne's bright future within the company, pointing out that as she begins to apply her new skills to projects, she will gain invaluable experience that could only enhance her career trajectory. He mentioned that this year's appraisal was a recognition of her past achievements and a vote of confidence in her future contributions. Raghu's perspective offered a reminder of the long-term benefits of Anne's development and the company's commitment to recognizing her evolving role and expertise.

Jasmeet got where Raghu was coming from, but he could not help worrying about his own role. He was the one who had to face his team members, who were often disappointed by their raises. Jasmeet's job was to explain the company's salary decisions and help his team see where they stood, but this was tough. He found himself in this spot many times, and sometimes, he was not even sure himself about the reasons behind the appraisal outcomes. It felt like he was just the messenger, passing along information from the higher-ups without being fully convinced about it himself. This made it hard for him to convincingly explain things to his team, as he was caught in the middle, trying to make sense of the company's policies and his team's hopes. Jasmeet, filled with many thoughts, went back to his desk, and called Anne. Anne was hopeful this time. She thought that after she talked about her hard work to Jasmeet and HR, they would definitely listen to her concerns. What she did not know was that Jasmeet already had a gentle way of explaining that she would need to wait another year for any possible changes.

When Anne talked to Jasmeet, she did not feel better about the situation. The conversation did not lessen her worries or make her feel more positive about her circumstances. Anne was particularly concerned about the size of her salary increase, believing it did not reflect the amount of hard work she had put into her job. As a result of this conversation and her concerns about the raise, Anne began to feel uncertain about her position and prospects within the company. She started to question whether she had a future there, given her perception that her efforts were not being adequately recognized or rewarded. This feeling made her start to pull away from her job.

She went to talk to her friend Raman about not wanting to stay with the company anymore. While drinking coffee, Raman was curious and asked, "Anne, how much was your raise?" He was surprised to find out Anne got a bigger raise than he did, probably because she worked hard in all areas, and her managers did notice her efforts. But even with this news, Anne still felt like her work was not valued enough, and she thought about looking for a new job.

When someone starts feeling negative about where they are, that is when they begin looking for better opportunities elsewhere. This feeling usually comes from being frustrated or unhappy with their current situation. That is the moment they start thinking about making a change and finding a new place where they can grow. It is like deciding to sail in a different boat to see if it takes them to a better place. Anne decided that it was time for a change. With her mind made up to leave, she began taking steps to make her decision a reality.

Key observations from this chapter –

Understanding the Appraisal Process: Anne's experience underscores the importance of understanding how appraisals work within an organization. Employees should seek clarity on the factors that influence increments and promotions, including performance metrics, organizational budget constraints, and market conditions.

Value of Continuous Learning: Anne's determination to acquire new skills and her decision to pivot towards a more in-demand technology highlight the critical role continuous learning plays in career advancement. Staying updated with industry trends and enhancing one's skill set can open new opportunities and lead to better compensation.

Communication is Key: The story illustrates the importance of open communication between employees and their managers. Sharing concerns, asking for feedback, and discussing career aspirations can help manage expectations and foster a supportive work environment.

Importance of Resilience: Facing disappointment in increments is part of the professional journey. Anne's resilience in the face of dissatisfaction with her raise teaches employees the value of perseverance and using setbacks as motivation to strive for greater achievements.

The Impact of Comparison: Comparing oneself with colleagues, as Anne did with Raman, can lead to feelings of inadequacy or unfairness. Employees should focus on their individual growth paths and understand that compensation can vary based on varied factors, including skill sets and organizational priorities.

Proactive Career Planning: Anne's proactive approach to her career, especially her strategic decision to gain certification in a niche technology, underscores the importance of planning for one's professional development. Setting clear career goals and actively working towards them can help employees navigate their growth more effectively.

Seeking Support: Engaging with mentors and leveraging the support of colleagues, as Anne did, can provide valuable insights and guidance. A fanatical support network can offer encouragement and advice, which is especially beneficial during times of uncertainty or career transitions.

Understanding Your Value: Anne's journey reflects the importance of understanding and articulating one's value to the organization. Being able to demonstrate how one's work contributes to the company's goals can strengthen the case for recognition and reward.

Balancing Professional and Personal Growth: Anne's commitment to her family and her career illustrates the balance many employees strive to achieve between professional success and personal fulfillment. Recognizing the importance of both aspects can help employees make more informed decisions about their career paths.

The Role of Self-Advocacy: Anne's willingness to express her dissatisfaction and seek better opportunities elsewhere highlights the importance of self-advocacy in the workplace. Employees should feel empowered to speak up for themselves and pursue the recognition and opportunities they believe they deserve.

CHAPTER 3

Conversations at the Crossroads

"Change is hard at first, messy in the middle and gorgeous
at the end"

– Robin Sharma

When a person sets their mind on accomplishing something, there is virtually no turning back. With an unobstructed vision of the desired outcome, individuals can carve their own paths toward achieving their goals. This principle was vividly illustrated in Anne's situation. Motivated by her determination to advance her career, she began to actively search for new opportunities, navigating through various job portals and leveraging social media to uncover potential openings in the industry. Despite this newfound focus on exploring other avenues, Anne remained committed to her current responsibilities, ensuring that her work and project deliveries were not compromised. However, the once-bright spark of enthusiasm that characterized her approach to tasks was noticeably dimmer. This change did not escape the attention of her colleagues or Jasmeet, her manager. They could see that while Anne continued to perform her duties, the passion and drive that used to inspire her work seemed to have faded. This shift signaled to those around her that Anne's professional aspirations might now lie beyond the confines of her current role, hinting at the deep-seated changes taking place within her as she pursued her goal of finding a role that better matched her ambitions and desired career trajectory.

Mobile rang. Anne grumbled softly to herself, a mix of irritation and bewilderment coloring her voice. "Why do these unknown numbers keep bothering me? It is as if my phone number is on display for the entire world to see. I just do not have the time to deal with this right now," she sighed, her frustration mounting as she hurried to get ready for work. Realizing she was running behind schedule, she decided to ignore the intrusive call, choosing instead to focus on making it to her vehicle and heading to the office without further delay.

Upon her arrival at work, Anne settled into her usual routine, which included a quick check of her phone. She discovered two missed calls from the same unfamiliar number she had dismissed earlier in her rush. Curiosity overtook her initial annoyance, prompting her to reconsider her stance on returning the call. "Who could be trying to reach me so urgently?" she wondered, the question nudging her towards action.

Dialing the mysterious number, she waited for a response. The call connected, and a voice on the other end inquired, "Who is calling?" Her patience worn thin, Anne could not help but respond with a hint of exasperation, "You're the one who called me several times, and now you're asking who I am? I'm Anne." Anne found herself engaging with the caller, her initial frustration giving way to a tentative curiosity about the reason behind these persistent attempts to contact her.

"Hello Anne. This is Spardha calling from jobportal.com. I came across your profile on our job portal site and wanted to have a chat with you. Are you currently considering a change in your job?" Spardha's words had an electrifying effect on Anne. She felt a surge of excitement and optimism, as if a door to new possibilities had suddenly opened. The idea that there might be opportunities out there for her to explore, potentially offering better compensation and career growth, filled her with hope.

"Could you give me just a moment, Spardha?" Anne responded; her voice tinged with eagerness. With these words, she quickly began to look around for a quiet spot—a secluded corner or an empty meeting room where she could talk freely and delve into the details of what Spardha might have to offer. This moment represented more than just a phone call; it was an encouragement of potential change in Anne's professional life, prompting her to step away from her routine environment to explore what lay on the horizon.

After finding a quiet room where she could speak privately, Anne resumed her conversation with Spardha. Spardha shared that there was an open position for an Associate Designer in Hyderabad, and she took the time to thoroughly explain the job responsibilities and what the company would expect from Anne. During the conversation, Spardha also inquired about why Anne was considering a change. Anne was open and honest in her response, stating that her main reason was the lack of satisfactory salary growth in her current position. This honesty set the tone for a candid discussion about what Anne was hoping to find in her next role. Spardha then asked Anne about her salary expectations for the new position. Fortunately, what Anne was looking for aligned perfectly with the offer for the Associate Designer role. This moment was a positive sign for Anne, indicating that the opportunity could meet her needs and possibly offer the change she was seeking. It was a reassuring conversation, suggesting that making the move could indeed be the right step forward for her career and financial well-being.

The time and energy Anne invested in acquiring new technological skills appeared to pale in comparison to her deep-seated desire for a higher income. This ambition drove her through the rigorous recruitment process, culminating in her successful selection for the position. The moment she received the news, Anne felt an unparalleled surge of excitement, as if she had been equipped with new wings to soar higher in her professional life. This opportunity not only symbolized a significant leap in her career but also offered a beacon of hope for addressing the financial difficulties her family endured.

Throughout the entire night following her acceptance, Anne was swept up in a whirlwind of enthusiasm about the prospect of starting this new chapter. Yet, beneath the surface of this excitement, there brewed a quiet storm of frustration—a frustration born from her current situation and the lack of recognition for her efforts and achievements. Anne harbored a strong desire to release these pent-up feelings, planning to share them candidly with Jasmeet, her manager, the following day.

Anne felt a surge of pride and accomplishment, setting her apart from her peers, as she successfully navigated her very first job transition interview. The thrill of this achievement filled her with an urge to share the news far and wide, yet, true to her character, she first chose to confide in her trusted friend Raman. His response was a mix of congratulations and caution, advising her to ponder her decision further. In response, Anne, lifted by her recent success, encouraged Raman, "You should consider making a move too, Raman. It's really the quickest way to advance financially."

Raman appreciated her suggestion but shared his own perspective, "I'm thinking of staying on for another year or two. I want to deepen my expertise in my current skill. It's this knowledge that will equip me for more complex challenges down the line." Anne realized that convincing Raman was not her path forward; instead, she felt compelled to discuss her thoughts with Jasmeet, their manager. She believed it was crucial for Jasmeet to understand the repercussions of insufficient salary increases on employees' loyalty and connection to the company.

With this conviction, Anne sought out Jasmeet, ready to communicate her decision. She hoped to highlight the importance of recognizing and rewarding employees' contributions as a means of maintaining trust and a strong team dynamic. Jasmeet had noticed a change in Anne's behavior since the last round of pay raises and had a feeling she might be planning something big. His intuition was spot on. Anne met with him to announce her decision to resign, explaining her reasons clearly. Jasmeet attempted once more to advise her, pointing out that it might be too soon for such a drastic step, especially considering the promising opportunities she had based on what she'd learned over the past year. However, Anne had made up her mind. Firm in her decision, she chose to leave the company. Following their conversation, Anne sent a formal resignation email to HR and began her notice period, ready to move on to the next chapter of her career.

Raman was not happy about Anne's decision to leave, not because she was getting a better salary somewhere else, but because he felt she was not seeing the bigger picture. During Anne's notice period, Raman tried a few times to change her mind, hoping she might cancel her resignation. He said to her, "Anne, consider staying just one more year.

It could really boost your confidence, especially once you start using the innovative technology you have learned on actual projects. Would waiting another year really ruin your family's financial situation? If your parents have been managing so far, I bet they would understand and support your decision to stay on for a bit longer if you explained it to them. They might even think it is a promising idea for you to gain more experience. Please think it over again."

Anne fully grasped the perspectives offered by both Raman and Jasmeet, recognizing the wisdom in their advice. Yet, beneath her understanding lay a complex mix of emotions—an unspoken frustration, the pressing needs of her family, and the allure of a significant salary increase elsewhere—each pulling her away from her current role. These factors, intertwined with her personal and professional aspirations, made it increasingly difficult for her to envision a future within the organization.

And so, the inevitable day came. Anne bid farewell to the company that had been her professional home for two years. She left not just with the experience she had gained but also with a tapestry of memories—some that brought a smile to her face and others that evoked a bittersweet sentiment. This departure marked a significant milestone in her career, one that encapsulated the growth she had achieved, the challenges she had faced, and the resolve with which she stepped forward into the next chapter of her professional journey.

In upcoming chapters, I will circle back to share more about the developments in Anne's career over the ensuing years. However, at this moment, it is crucial to highlight a common theme in the professional world: numerous individuals leave their jobs primarily due to salary concerns. Yet, often, this reason becomes secondary to more pressing issues.

Consider the story of Anjuman, another character who found himself discontented, not with the financial aspect of his job, but with the leadership above him. Anjuman held the position of Project Manager, leading a substantial team in a manner like Jasmeet, as described in a previous narrative. Despite his successes, Anjuman was part of a larger organizational structure and reported to his Assistant Vice President, Abhinav, revealing the inevitable layers of hierarchy within any company.

The following chapter delves into Anjuman's experiences, his challenges with senior leadership, and the lessons that can be drawn from his journey. It is an invitation to explore how Anjuman navigated his professional environment, the decisions he faced, and the broader implications for others in similar situations. Turn the page to immerse yourself in Anjuman's story and uncover the insights it holds for navigating leadership dynamics and career satisfaction.

Key observations from the chapter –

Proactive Career Management: Anne's story emphasizes the importance of taking charge of one's career. Proactively seeking new opportunities, upskilling, and being open to change are crucial for career advancement and personal growth.

Balancing Commitment with Aspirations: Despite her intention to move on, Anne maintained her commitment to her current role, ensuring her work quality did not diminish. This balance between meeting current responsibilities while exploring future opportunities is pivotal.

Communication of Career Goals: Anne's interaction with Spardha from the job portal and her subsequent discussions highlight the importance of clear communication regarding career aspirations, salary expectations, and reasons for seeking change.

Impact of Recognition and Compensation: Anne's decision to leave was significantly influenced by her dissatisfaction with salary growth. This underscores the impact of recognition and fair compensation on employee retention and satisfaction.

Importance of Exploring New Opportunities: The narrative shows the value of being open to exploring new opportunities that align better with one's career goals and compensation expectations. It illustrates how external offers can validate an employee's market worth.

Decision-Making Process: Anne's thorough decision-making process, from initial frustration to considering a new job offer, reflects the complexities involved in making career decisions. It involves weighing current dissatisfaction against the potential for growth and better compensation elsewhere.

Perspectives on Career Growth: Raman's and Jasmeet's reactions to Anne's decision provide different perspectives on career growth. While Anne seeks immediate financial improvement, Raman values depth of expertise and Jasmeet emphasizes patience. This diversity in viewpoints illustrates that career paths are not one-size-fits-all and depend on individual priorities and circumstances.

Challenges of Leadership: Jasmeet's role as a manager dealing with Anne's resignation highlights the challenges leaders face in balancing organizational constraints with the aspirations of their team members. Effective leadership involves understanding and addressing the concerns of team members to retain talent.

Personal vs. Professional Priorities: Anne's decision is also a reflection of the struggle to balance personal needs and professional ambitions. Her family's financial situation plays a significant role in her choice, showing how external factors can influence career decisions.

The Resignation Process: Anne's formal resignation and the notice period serve as a procedural insight into transitioning from one job to another. It shows the importance of maintaining professionalism and fulfilling obligations until the last day.

CHAPTER 4

The Silent Signals of Discontent

"Bad leaders care about who is right. Good leaders care about what is right"

– Simon Sinek

As Anjuman got ready for work at around 9 am, his wife called him over for breakfast. He joined her but seemed lost in thought, barely touching his food. Noticing his distraction, his wife asked, "Is everything okay, or are you having issues with Abhinav again?"

Anjuman sighed, acknowledging her observation. "You're right. I am not even looking forward to going to the office or seeing him," he confessed, clearly troubled by the thought.

With a concerned yet playful smile, his wife then asked, "Oh, again something happened with your boss, Abhinav? How long are you going to feel like this? Do you think waiting for Abhinav to leave will make things better?"

Her question made Anjuman think. It highlighted how he was stuck, waiting for something to change at work, instead of figuring out what he could do to improve his own situation. This simple breakfast conversation opened Anjuman's eyes to his current state and the need to consider his next steps more proactively.

"Not feeling much like joking around. Why would he leave just because I am having issues with him? But I get what you are saying," Anjuman responded to his wife, acknowledging her insight despite his frustration. "We'll talk more this evening," he added, suggesting they continue the conversation later as he prepared to face the day ahead.

As Anjuman drove to the office, memories of better times at the company began to surface, contrasting sharply with his current feelings of discontent. He found himself pondering why, two and a half years ago, he had been so eager to accept the offer from this company. Back then, he was eager for a senior role that matched his experience and landing this job had felt like a significant achievement. The early days, under Harry's leadership, were filled with a sense of camaraderie and support that now seemed lost. Anjuman recalled a particularly challenging time when his team could not deliver a project on schedule. Harry had been there for them, not just offering moral support but also stepping in to communicate with the client, highlighting his leadership and empathy.

That period marked the beginning of Anjuman's deep professional respect for Harry, a sentiment that remained even after Harry had moved on from the company. The connection they shared was not just about work; it was about mutual respect and understanding, qualities that Anjuman still valued and found in his conversations with Harry, who always responded with the same grace and warmth.

Caught in this wave of nostalgia and reflection, Anjuman hardly noticed the journey passing by, nor the usual traffic snarls that would have frustrated him on any other day. Before he knew it, he had arrived at the office parking lot, his mind still wrapped in thoughts of the past and what had changed since then.

At work, Anjuman quickly got busy with his usual tasks. But during lunch, he took a break to eat and chat with his friend Albert. They had become good friends over the last two and a half years, often sharing lunch and talking about work. Albert was also a Project Manager but worked under a different boss. During their lunches, they would talk about how their bosses were doing and the kind of support they got from them. Ever since Anjuman's favorite boss, Harry, left the company, Anjuman missed having a supportive leader. He often thought about how nice it would be to work in Albert's team, where he might find the kind of leadership he was looking for. This idea kept growing stronger, especially when he remembered the good times and support he had when Harry was around.

During lunch, Albert noticed Anjuman seemed a bit off and asked him about the problems he was facing with his current boss, wondering why Anjuman felt uneasy working under him.

Anjuman took a moment to gather his thoughts before replying, "You know, Albert, there's a big difference between genuinely trusting your team and just pretending to trust them. When you really trust your team, it shows in your actions and how you treat them. But if you are only acting like you trust them without meaning it, people can realize. That's one of the biggest issues I'm dealing with." Anjuman's explanation highlighted the core of his discomfort: the lack of genuine trust and support from his boss, which made his work environment challenging.

Driven by curiosity, Albert pressed further, "But why do you feel that Abhinav only pretends to trust the team? What makes you say the trust is not genuine?"

Anjuman sighed, knowing the complexity of his feelings could not be easily unpacked. "It's hard to pinpoint everything, but I'll give you an example. When I assign tasks to my team, I make sure they have all they need to succeed without any obstacles. I am there to support them, not to micromanage. My communication with the team is always clear and open. They know what their responsibilities are, and they also know I have their back, whether that means advocating for their needs with management or with our clients. This builds real trust between us, making it easier to manage our workload effectively.

"Moreover, I am mindful of their work-life balance. Pushing the team too hard might get short-term results, but it is a surefire way to lose their trust and respect eventually," Anjuman added, illustrating his approach to leadership.

Albert nodded, absorbing Anjuman's perspective. "You'd think these principles would be obvious to anyone in a leadership position. If these are the issues you're facing, I can see why you're struggling."

He continued, reflecting on his own experiences, "My boss and I always try to ensure that no one feels compelled to leave over such fundamental management failures. We might not always control salary adjustments, but we can certainly influence how valued and supported our team feels. Research shows that while salary is a key factor in job satisfaction, the impact of uncaring or uninspiring leaders should not be underestimated. It's often these leadership failures that drive good employees away, preventing them from having a fulfilling career within an organization."

The discussion between Anjuman and Albert was getting deeper and more engaging. Albert, puzzled, shared his thoughts, "I really don't get why people like Abhinav act the way they do. Don't they realize that their behavior affects the whole team's work and morale? Sure, on paper, everything might look fine with deadlines met and goals achieved, but at what cost? In the end, leaders like that end up losing the most important thing: respect from their team. They might act friendly to your face, but you must watch out for what they do behind your back. If they cannot be trusted to support their team properly, you also must be careful about taking their words at face value. Such personalities could let you down or turn against you at any moment."

Albert's words reflected a deeper understanding of the delicate dynamics of trust and respect in the workplace, emphasizing the importance of genuine leadership and the consequences of its absence.

Anjuman shared with Albert another insight, emphasizing the importance of mutual support within a team, regardless of whether members are junior or senior. He believes that everyone on the team holds specific responsibilities, commitments, and accountabilities toward their work. However, Anjuman is convinced that the path to fulfilling these duties becomes smoother with the backing of someone in a senior position. His aspiration is to be seen as a mentor by his team, someone who can coach and offer guidance as needed, creating an environment where open discussions are welcomed. Anjuman stresses that his leadership style avoids leveraging his position to simply exert authority over his team members.

He pointed out that in the workplace, mistakes are inevitable and can sometimes complicate matters. Instead of resorting to reprimands or fostering negative views, which can erode trust, a more constructive approach is required. This perspective highlights a significant disparity between his management style and that of Abhinav. Anjuman feels that Abhinav acts more like a watchdog, focusing on oversight and reporting to higher-ups without really engaging with the team's actual challenges or offering the necessary guidance. Just as Anjuman's team looks up to him for his experience and mentorship, he, too, seeks similar support from Abhinav. This gap in expectations and reality underlines the contrast in their approaches to leadership and teamwork.

Albert, intrigued by the dynamics between Anjuman and his boss, posed a question laden with curiosity, "Does this mean you're expecting Abhinav to be constantly at your side assisting, for you to regard him in the same light as Harry?"

Anjuman, keen to set the record straight, interjected with clarification, "It's not about requiring Abhinav's intervention on every matter. My frustration stems from his perpetual stance of 'ownership' and the expectation that I alone should find solutions in situations where I lack control. Seeking guidance from him has often left me wanting. If he is uncertain of the answer, I would appreciate a collaborative effort to brainstorm solutions rather than facing his authoritative insistence that I shoulder the entire burden. I am fully committed to my responsibilities and capable of navigating challenges as they arise. However, just as my team turns to me for leadership, there are times I look to Abhinav for direction."

He continued to elaborate on his preference for Harry's leadership style, "What set Harry apart was his innate ability to mentor and coach, offering his support unconditionally. He had a nurturing and motivational presence that made all of us feel valued and driven to excel. Harry's approach to leadership was not just about overseeing work; it was about actively contributing to our growth and success. That's the essence of the leadership I admire and yearn for in Abhinav." Anjuman's words painted a vivid picture of his ideal work environment—one where leadership is characterized by empathy, support, and a mutual commitment to solving problems together.

No matter the reason for seeking a new job, the conversation about salary expectations inevitably comes up, whether you are updating your profile on a job portal or talking directly to a recruiter. Despite numerous factors motivating a job change, the desire for a salary increase is common among most people. For some, it might be the main reason, while for others, it ranks second or third. However, the prospect of earning more money remains an underlying motive for many. In Anjuman's situation, as he explored new job opportunities, he faced this very question from a recruiter.

Anjuman expressed his desire for "more responsibilities and a chance to lead larger teams." While this was true, deep down, he was also motivated by other factors he chose not to disclose—specifically, his current boss's lack of effective leadership. He remembered an interview he and HR had conducted with a candidate who openly criticized their Lead for focusing more on management than on mentorship. Anjuman had silently agreed with the candidate's assessment but also noted that HR dismissed the candidate for what they perceived as a poor attitude.

To avoid being judged similarly, Anjuman carefully steered clear of criticizing his boss directly when discussing his reasons for wanting to leave. Instead, he focused on his professional aspirations. He did not ignore the salary question, either; he made sure to discuss his salary expectations with the recruiter, balancing his desire for career growth with his financial goals. This strategic approach allowed Anjuman to navigate the delicate conversation without casting himself in a negative light, all while keeping his real motivations and concerns in mind.

After successfully navigating through several rounds of interviews, Anjuman received an offer for a senior position at another company. While the salary increase was certainly a perk, the real joy for him came from the relief of leaving behind the stressful environment created by his current boss. He felt as though he was finally breaking free from constraints that had held him back. It is often said that the notice period feels like a honeymoon period for employees, especially in situations like Anjuman's, where leaving feels like liberation from captivity.

Anjuman approached Abhinav's office with a newfound sense of confidence and fearlessness, unburdened by any concerns about potential criticisms or issues Abhinav might raise. His stride was steady and his resolve firm, reflecting his readiness to confront whatever lay ahead. Abhinav, on his part, was anticipating a strict discussion about certain reports he expected from Anjuman. He had presumed Anjuman's visit would solely focus on this pending task, showing minimal interest in engaging in conversations beyond the immediate scope of work. As Anjuman entered the cabin, the atmosphere was charged with unspoken anticipation. Abhinav, preoccupied with the expectation of discussing the reports, was momentarily oblivious to the shift in Anjuman's demeanor. This moment marked a significant turning point for Anjuman, who was prepared to navigate the conversation with a level of assertiveness and clarity he had previously restrained. The dynamic between the two was poised for a change, with Anjuman ready to address matters beyond just the day-to-day tasks, signaling his readiness to engage in deeper, more meaningful dialogue about the work environment and leadership style.

As soon as Anjuman stepped into the cabin, Abhinav, assuming the purpose of the visit, inquired, "Oh, have you finished what I asked for and come to talk about it? Unfortunately, I cannot meet you right now. Can you come back in an hour?"

Anjuman, unphased by the misunderstanding, responded calmly, "Sure, I can meet you after an hour. However, my visit isn't about the report."

This response left Abhinav with a puzzled look on his face, his initial assumptions disrupted. "Then, what do you wish to discuss?" he asked, a hint of apprehension in his voice.

With a newfound assertiveness bolstered by his confidence, Anjuman responded with a touch of aggression, "Abhinav, there are aspects of our work where your advice would be invaluable, given your seniority and deeper understanding of management's plans. Unfortunately, I have felt a disconnect in that support. Regardless, that is not why I am here today. I have come to tell you personally that I have decided to resign. I believe it's important to have this conversation before I submit my official resignation."

This direct approach marked a pivotal moment in Anjuman's professional journey, as he articulated his decision to leave, underlining the significance of addressing his concerns directly with Abhinav before making his departure official. Upon hearing Anjuman's intention to resign, Abhinav immediately halted his other tasks, shifting his full attention to the conversation at hand. He was taken aback by Anjuman's decision and became intent on persuading him to reconsider. It is a rare occurrence for someone to retract their resignation once their mind is made up, yet Abhinav hoped to be an exception to this rule. Despite his efforts, Anjuman proceeded with his decision and submitted his resignation letter.

Abhinav had always valued having a competent and effective team member like Anjuman and wanted to maintain that strength within his team. However, he failed to recognize in time how his own leadership style, marked by a lack of care and inspiration, was adversely affecting the emotional well-being and job satisfaction of his team members, including Anjuman. This oversight led to a situation where even his sincere attempt to reverse Anjuman's decision was unsuccessful, highlighting the profound impact leadership can have on team dynamics and individual career choices.

Employees who feel trapped or undervalued are unlikely to speak positively about their experiences. In the current era, individuals who are considering changing jobs often investigate a company's work environment and values by looking at social media platforms or asking their personal and professional contacts for insights. Because of this, if a company has received negative reviews or feedback—whether about its culture, leadership, or any other aspect—this information can spread widely and quickly. As a result, the company might face challenges in attracting new talent, as potential employees are deterred by the negative perceptions they encounter during their research. Everyone desires to work in an environment free from undue stress, where they can concentrate on their tasks and pursue growth. If you find yourself under the leadership of bosses like Abhinav, it is essential to take lessons from such experiences. Remember, you always have the option to move on from such situations. However, equally important is reflecting on these experiences to ensure that when you're in a position to lead, you don't replicate the same behaviors. Learn how to manage your teams effectively, fostering an atmosphere of support and understanding. Aim to be the leader who inspires and motivates, not one from whom your team seeks to escape. This approach not only benefits your professional development but also contributes to a healthier, more productive workplace culture.

Despite the differences in jobs, cultural backgrounds, and workplace environments across various countries, global workforce trends reveal a commonality in the needs and aspirations of workers worldwide. At the core of a successful and productive work environment is the universal desire among employees for a sense of belonging, recognition, and fulfillment in their professional roles. As highlighted by research from the Harvard Business Review, employee productivity and engagement significantly increase when their four fundamental needs—physical, emotional, mental, and spiritual—are adequately met. This comprehensive approach to employee well-being not only enhances individual satisfaction but also contributes to the overall performance and output of a company. Furthermore, studies have established a strong link between the level of employee engagement and the success of a business, underscoring the importance of addressing these needs to foster a motivated and efficient workforce.

Quiet quitting, if not addressed with deliberate and targeted actions, can act as a "silent killer," negatively affecting both employees' earnings and the overall performance of a company. This phenomenon, where employees disengage and do only the minimum required work, can stealthily undermine the vitality of a workplace. Without proactive measures to counteract its impact, quiet quitting can lead to decreased productivity, lower morale, and ultimately harm both individual career growth and organizational success.

Key observations from this chapter –

Voice Your Concerns: Anjuman's situation underscores the importance of communicating your concerns and aspirations with management. Keeping silent about your dissatisfaction or ambitions only leads to frustration and missed opportunities for resolution or advancement.

Assess Leadership Style and Support: The impact of leadership style on your job satisfaction cannot be overstated. If you are under a management style that does not align with your values or support your growth, it is crucial to recognize this as a potential factor in your overall job satisfaction.

Reflect on What You Value in Leadership: Anjuman's admiration for Harry's leadership style highlights the importance of working under management that inspires and supports you. Reflect on the qualities you value in a leader and seek them out in your career.

Be Prepared to Make Difficult Decisions: Ultimately, Anjuman's decision to resign after years of service is a testament to the importance of being prepared to leave if an organization can no longer meet your career needs. It is a difficult but sometimes necessary step for personal and professional growth.

Research Potential Employers: Before moving to a new organization, research its culture, leadership style, and growth opportunities, much like you would consider a company's financial offer. This can prevent repeating past dissatisfaction and ensure a better fit for your career aspirations.

Self-Growth is Key: Remember, your career is a journey of self-growth. Like Anjuman, you may seek environments that challenge you and offer opportunities for learning and advancement. Always prioritize your development and well-being in your career choices.

CHAPTER 5

Beyond Titles and Tenure

"Boredom is a great motivator"

– Uma Thurman

In the narratives of Anne and Anjuman, we observe distinct motivations driving their career decisions. Anne was primarily focused on financial growth, seeking opportunities that would enhance her earnings. On the other hand, Anjuman's dissatisfaction stemmed from dealing with an uncaring supervisor, highlighting a different aspect of workplace discontent. Beyond these individual cases, there exist broader considerations that people consider, such as the potential for expanding their knowledge base and advancing their career paths. While the reasons for considering a job change may overlap across different domains—be it financial, managerial dissatisfaction, or professional development—the ultimate decision to resign and enter into a notice period often comes down to a critical point of acute discomfort or severe frustration. This tipping point is highly personal and varies from one individual to another, reflecting the culmination of unresolved issues or unmet needs that make the current position untenable, prompting the move towards seeking a more fulfilling and supportive work environment.

A few decades ago, it was common to see individuals begin their careers in humble positions like peons and retire as head clerks. This career trajectory was feasible primarily because the organization provided opportunities for growth. The desire to advance and acquire new skills is fundamental to human nature, fueling individuals to embrace diverse responsibilities as time progresses. However, this path to growth hinges on the availability of such opportunities within the workplace.

When someone spends many years at a single organization, focusing solely on a specific type of task, they might find themselves in a comfortable but limiting situation. The longer they remain in this static role without diversifying their skills or tackling new challenges, the harder it becomes for them to adapt to changes or embrace learning opportunities. This scenario underscores a crucial aspect of career development: the environment in which one works plays a significant role in determining one's ability to grow and evolve professionally. Without the chance to step into new roles or projects, even the most aspiring individuals might find themselves stuck, unable to fully realize their potential due to the lack of conducive conditions for growth.

After transitioning to a new organization, Anjuman spent good time there for almost six years and tomorrow he is planning to resign. He was thinking "Moving from an earlier organization because of Abhinav was a good decision. At that time, I was thinking of a good environment, and I got it. But I never thought from the angle that one day I will leave this because of no growth."

"Please come to the dining table for dinner," his wife called him for dinner. "So, you have made up your mind to resign tomorrow? I think you have no problem working here but you are not seeing any change in the work. Right?" she asked while serving food to him.

Anjuman expressed his agreement by nodding his head. He further added, "It seems to be monotonous work because there are only two levels above me where I can progress. And at higher levels movement is extremely critical as positions hardly anyone would like to leave." He further explained, "As I am looking for various responsibilities, I cannot work for the same work for many years. That uneasiness was the reason to plan to resign."

But why did you not think about this point earlier? His wife asked.

"During that time, I was experiencing financial growth, enjoyed his roles, and felt aligned with the company's management. However, as time passed, I began to ponder my prospects within the organization." Anjuman justified to her wife.

Continuing discussion with her wife Anjuman added, "I was in a dilemma common to many in senior positions, especially within mid-sized companies: the question of "what next?" Despite my achievements and current high-level position, I realized lately that opportunities for further promotion were limited. In such organizations, there simply are not as many roles as possible or positions available at the top, making it challenging for those at senior levels to find pathways for advancement beyond a certain point."

"Oh, so earlier you were enjoying it and later you started realizing that something was not aligned with your profile. Was that so? Even four years back you were promoted also as a senior project manager" Wife exclaimed.

Anjuman recalled the promotion he received four years prior, which elevated him from the role of Project Manager to Senior Project Manager.

As he shared this memory with his wife, a smile tinged his words, "The most notable change seemed to be the title itself, and practically nothing more. That shift in designation was warmly celebrated across social media, where my transition from PM to Sr. PM attracted an outpouring of congratulatory messages and optimistic wishes. Many echoed the sentiment that 'the sky's the limit.' However, sitting here today, reflecting on those words, I find them somewhat disconnected from the reality of my position."

His wife, curious, asked, "So, does this mean people don't really get promoted much at your place? Do they stay in the same job from when they start to when they leave?"

Anjuman quickly corrected her, "Oh, it's not like that. People who start in the lower or junior positions do have chances to grow. They can get promoted to higher positions based on how well they do their jobs. But the real problem is for those of us in the higher positions, especially in a mid-sized company like where I work."

He wanted to make sure his wife understood that while there is a path upwards for those at the start of their careers, moving up becomes tougher for those already at the top, particularly in smaller or mid-sized companies where there are fewer positions to move into.

"Hopefully, we won't run into this situation again. I'm assuming the new company you're considering is a larger one, where you'll find more opportunities for ongoing learning and development?" His wife sought confirmation, hoping that Anjuman's next move would offer him the career growth and opportunities he was looking for. She expressed her hope that a larger organization might provide a broader scope for advancement and personal development, avoiding the stagnation he experienced previously.

"Yes, that's correct. The new company is indeed larger, with more people, a variety of roles, and numerous positions available. My issue is not really with the size of an organization whether it is small or midsize. The crux of the matter lies in whether an organization possesses a clear agenda for growth and engagement that caters to every employee. For anyone who has a strong desire to learn and work, such an environment can be fulfilling. It is crucial for organizations to have a vision that sustains and nurtures the employees' interest in their work over the time," Anjuman elaborated, sharing his perspective on what makes a workplace engaging and conducive to growth.

"I get it, Anjuman," his wife responded, showing her understanding. She continued, "This uncertainty about where your career is heading has left you feeling stuck, hasn't it? Even though becoming a Senior Project Manager sounds impressive, it did not really change your day-to-day work much from when you were a Project Manager. That must be confusing. It's like, if someone were to ask you how your job as a Sr. PM is different from when you were just a PM, it sounds like you'd have a hard time pointing out any significant changes." Her words empathetically acknowledged the crux of Anjuman's professional dissatisfaction, highlighting the disconnect between the expectation of growth associated with a promotion and the reality of unchanged responsibilities.

Anjuman's journey led him to a profound understanding, shaped by experience: that true wisdom comes from navigating the intricacies of one's career path. He pondered whether, for some in management, altering job titles without corresponding changes in responsibilities might merely be a superficial tactic. Such a strategy, he hypothesized, could be aimed at creating a front of progression, where the excitement of a new designation masks the stagnation of growth opportunities. This approach, while potentially boosting morale in the short term, might leave employees blissfully unaware of the lack of substantive development in their roles.

The following day, Anjuman scheduled a meeting with his manager, Tanay, who was the head of their cluster and oversaw a capable team, including Anjuman. During their interaction, Anjuman sensed a shared concern among his colleagues about the future of their careers. There was a palpable feeling of restlessness regarding growth opportunities within the organization. Anjuman was certain that once any of his team members received a chance to advance their career outside the company, they would not hesitate to leave. This realization underscored a broader issue within the team – a collective yearning for progression and the inevitable outcome of losing talented individuals if their aspirations for growth were not addressed.

Anjuman took the opportunity to share his thoughts and feelings with Tanay, laying out his reasons for considering resignation. Tanay, taken aback by this revelation, expressed his surprise. He had been unaware of any dissatisfaction Anjuman might have been experiencing, either with his specific role or with the organization. Tanay questioned Anjuman, saying, "I had no idea you were facing any issues with your work or with the company. Why would you want to leave? You are an invaluable asset to us." Tanay's response highlighted his recognition of Anjuman's contributions and his concern over losing such a pivotal member of the team, signaling a moment of realization about the importance of understanding and addressing the needs and aspirations of his employees.

Anjuman expressed his gratitude to Tanay for his kind words and appreciation, clarifying, "Thank you, Tanay, for recognizing my efforts. My decision is not driven by dissatisfaction with anyone here. It's about my personal desire for growth and the need for new opportunities or platforms that can facilitate that growth."

Tanay, seeking clarity, asked, "So, are you saying the work you're doing isn't challenging enough?"

Anjuman elaborated, "The work itself is fine, but it has become repetitive for me. I am asking myself, 'What new things can I learn here?' My goal is to advance within my area of expertise, but that's become difficult because the company doesn't offer a variety of work, I need to further develop my skills."

Tanay fully grasped the essence of Anjuman's concerns. It dawned on him that Anjuman's issue was deeply rooted in the limitations of the organization's capacity to provide diverse and challenging opportunities for its employees. Tanay recognized the significance of Anjuman's point: the organization lacked a solution to cater to the growth aspirations of employees like Anjuman, underscoring a broader challenge that needed addressing.

Any organization can play a vital role here to avoid such resignations and pushing an employee into notice period tenure. Below is some suggestive approach for an organization –

Provide Clear Growth Pathways: Organizations should ensure that employees at all levels have a transparent and achievable path for growth. This is particularly crucial for mid – to senior-level positions, where opportunities may become less apparent.

Align Promotions with Role Expansion: Anjuman's experience of receiving a promotion in title only, without an expansion of responsibilities, serves as a cautionary tale. Promotions should be meaningful, accompanied by new challenges and learning opportunities to keep employees engaged and motivated.

Encourage Continuous Learning: The aspiration for self-growth and development is innate. Organizations should cultivate an environment that encourages continuous learning and skill diversification, enabling employees to remain adaptable and engaged.

Recognize and Address Monotony: Acknowledging Anjuman's sense of monotony in his role underscores the need for job roles to evolve. Keeping work challenging and varied can help prevent feelings of stagnation.

Understand Employee Aspirations: Regular discussions about career goals and aspirations can help management align organizational needs with individual growth paths, ensuring that talented employees like Anjuman see a future within the company.

Promote from Within: Demonstrating a commitment to promoting from within can motivate employees to invest in their professional development, knowing that their efforts can lead to upward mobility within the organization.

Maintain Open Lines of Communication: Tanay's surprise at Anjuman's resignation highlights the importance of open communication. Regular check-ins can surface concerns and aspirations before they lead to decisions to leave.

Offer Diverse Work Opportunities: Especially in larger organizations, providing a variety of projects and roles can help employees like Anjuman find new areas of interest and growth within the same company, reducing the urge to look elsewhere for fulfillment.

For employees navigating their career paths, the experience of Anjuman offers valuable insights into managing professional growth, job satisfaction, and transitions. Here are some key suggestions for employees:

Evaluate Growth Opportunities: Before accepting a job offer or deciding to stay in a role, assess the opportunities for growth within the organization. Ensure that there is a clear path for advancement that aligns with your career goals.

Seek Meaningful Promotions: Advocate for promotions that come with genuine increases in responsibility and learning opportunities, not just title changes. This ensures that your career progression is both rewarding and substantive.

Communicate with Management: Maintain open lines of communication with your supervisors about your career aspirations, challenges, and needs for support. This can help align your goals with organizational opportunities.

Embrace Continuous Learning: Actively seek opportunities for learning and skill development, both within and outside your current role. This proactive approach can make you more adaptable and valuable in a rapidly changing job market.

Be Prepared for Monotony: Recognize that some level of repetition and monotony can occur in any job. Develop strategies to stay engaged, such as taking on new projects, mentoring others, or learning new skills related to your field. But if for long it is repetitive, look for other options.

Plan for Long-Term Career Goals: Regularly revisit and update your career goals. Planning for the long term can help you make strategic decisions about job changes, additional education, or shifts in your career focus.

Network Within and Outside Your Organization: Building a broad professional network can provide insights into other career paths, introduce you to new opportunities, and offer support during transitions.

Assess Organizational Culture: Consider the culture of potential employers and their alignment with your values and needs for support. A positive, growth-oriented culture can enhance job satisfaction.

Be Ready to Move On: If your current organization cannot offer the growth, learning, or environment you seek, be prepared to explore opportunities elsewhere. Staying in a stagnant role can hinder your professional development.

CHAPTER 6

In Pursuit of Alignment

"Work gives you meaning, and purpose and life is empty without it"

– Stephen Hawking

Mayank, deeply engrossed in his current project, felt a wave of frustration wash over him as another message from Amit appeared on his screen, signaling yet another assignment. As a Group Leader at a prominent insurance company, he was tasked with orchestrating the efforts of area sales managers, aligning their strategies, and steering the team towards substantial business growth. Under Amit's supervision, his reporting manager, Mayank's responsibilities were expansive, demanding a fine balance between strategic oversight and hands-on involvement in day-to-day operations.

The role, inherently challenging and fulfilling, had lately become a source of discontent for Mayank. The assignments handed down by Amit seemed increasingly disconnected from the core objectives they were supposed to meet. Each new task felt like a detour from the strategic initiatives Mayank believed were crucial for driving business growth. This latest assignment was no exception. As he clicked open Amit's message, Mayank could not help but question the rationale behind these seemingly arbitrary tasks.

"Why does Amit keep diverting my focus with these assignments?" Mayank pondered, his mind racing with thoughts of the strategic projects he was eager to push forward, those that truly aligned with the company's growth ambitions. It was becoming harder to see the value in these distractions, which pulled him further away from the goals he was passionate about achieving.

In his role as a Group Leader, Mayank had always prided himself on his ability to bridge the efforts of different sales managers, creating a cohesive strategy that leveraged their collective strengths for the greater good of the company. His vision for the team was clear: to innovate, to challenge the status quo, and to drive growth in a competitive market. Yet, the continuous stream of unrelated assignments from Amit was diluting his focus, leaving him questioning the impact of his contribution.

As Mayank stared at his computer screen, a sense of determination began to take hold. It was time to address the growing misalignment between his role's intended purpose and the reality of his day-to-day tasks. The disconnect was not only a source of personal frustration but a potential barrier to the team's success. Mayank realized that for the sake of his team's morale and the company's objectives, he needed to have a candid conversation with Amit. It was essential to realign his assignments with the strategic goals that truly mattered, to ensure that his role as a Group Leader was both meaningful and effective in contributing to the company's growth trajectory.

In the bustling office space, Mayank found a moment of camaraderie with Nayan, a fellow Group Leader overseeing a different team but sharing the same reporting line with Amit. Both seasoned in their roles, they found common ground in their experiences under Amit's management, particularly when it came to the allocation of tasks that seemed misaligned with their skills and the core objectives of their positions. These tasks, often perceived as peripheral or even trivial, had become a recurring theme, detracting from their primary responsibilities and, by extension, their teams' performance.

Nayan, with a tone of shared frustration, echoed Mayank's sentiments, "These assignments, they're pulling us away from what truly matters. It's not just about the time they consume; it's the focus they divert from our real work, the work that drives growth and impacts our bottom line." His words resonated with Mayank, underscoring the disconnect between the tasks handed down by Amit and the strategic goals they were committed to achieving.

The conversation shifted as Mayank, fueled by a sense of resolve, confided in Nayan, "This time, I'll handle it. But if this continues, I cannot just stand by. I'll need to have a word with Amit." His voice was low, a whisper almost, but it carried the weight of a decision made. Mayank was prepared to step into Amit's cabin and articulate the dissonance between the tasks being assigned and the expertise and interests of his team. He recognized the importance of aligning work with the team's growth objectives, not only for the sake of efficiency but also for maintaining morale and motivation.

Mayank's resolve to address the issue was not just about advocating for his own interests; it was about safeguarding the productivity and engagement of his team. The term 'thankless job' had come to symbolize the frustration of being stuck in work that seemed to offer little in terms of professional development or recognition. It was a sentiment that both he and Nayan shared, a recognition that their capacity to contribute meaningfully was being undermined by the very tasks that were meant to fill their days.

As they parted ways, Mayank's thoughts were a mix of apprehension and determination. The conversation with Amit loomed in his mind, a necessary confrontation to realign their work with the company's strategic vision. It was a step he was ready to take, supported by the knowledge that in doing so, he was not only advocating for his own professional growth but also for the collective success of his team and, ultimately, the company.

Over time, Mayank found himself increasingly burdened with tasks that fell outside the scope of his role as a Group Leader, particularly in logistics—a field in which he had little expertise or interest. These assignments seemed disconnected from his primary goal of driving business growth alongside the area sales managers. The accumulation of such tasks not only diverted his attention from crucial responsibilities but also sparked a sense of frustration and discontent within him.

Determined to address the issue, Mayank sought a direct conversation with Amit, his reporting manager. Walking into Amit's cabin, he carried with him a mix of apprehension and the hope for a constructive resolution. As he stood before Amit, Mayank articulated his concerns with a blend of honesty and professionalism. "Amit, I've been reflecting on the work you've been assigning to me recently, and I feel it's important to share that these logistic tasks aren't aligning with my strengths or my role's objectives," he began, his tone firm yet respectful.

Mayank continued, "I believe there are others within our team, perhaps a coordinator, who possess the specific skill set and expertise required for these logistic assignments. They could handle these tasks more effectively and efficiently than I can." His suggestion was not merely a plea for relief from the work he found burdensome, but a practical solution aimed at optimizing team resources and ensuring that each task was matched with the appropriate skill set.

Upon hearing Mayank's concerns, Amit responded with a perspective that reflected the broader expectations of the organization from its leaders. "Mayank, as a group leader, the organization trusts you with a range of responsibilities, not limited to specific tasks. It's about fulfilling what is required and necessary for our collective success," Amit began, emphasizing the flexible nature of leadership roles.

He continued, addressing the issue of resource allocation, "Currently, we're operating without coordinators, which indeed places additional demands on our existing team members. Given the circumstances, I believe you are capable of handling these tasks. It's not just about who is the best fit for the job but about who is available and can adapt to meet our needs."

Amit acknowledged the challenge but also expressed confidence in Mayank's abilities. "If you need some time to familiarize yourself with these new responsibilities, that's understandable. Take the time you need to learn, but I encourage you to embrace this as an opportunity to broaden your skill set and demonstrate leadership versatility."

Amit's response caught Mayank off guard, stirring a mix of frustration and disappointment within him. Mayank had always thrived in his role as a Group Leader, engaging with the challenges that came with it and driving towards the business's growth with enthusiasm. However, the additional tasks that resembled those of a coordinator seemed misaligned with his career aspirations and skill set, sparking a sense of disillusionment about his responsibilities.

Confronted with Amit's stance, Mayank felt compelled to clarify his position, hoping to find a middle ground. "I understand the need for flexibility and stepping up when the situation calls for it," Mayank started, trying to balance his commitment to the team with his personal career goals. "I'm fully committed to taking on any challenges or additional responsibilities that align with my role as a Group Leader. I'm more than willing to expand my workload in that direction."

However, Mayank also felt it necessary to set boundaries regarding tasks that he perceived as not contributing to his professional growth or the strategic objectives he was passionate about. "But concerning the coordinator-type tasks, I honestly feel they don't leverage my strengths or the leadership capabilities I aim to develop further. While I'm willing to support these needs temporarily, I believe it's in the best interest of both my professional development and the team's efficiency that this does not extend beyond a month." Mayank's response highlighted his willingness to support the organization's immediate needs while also expressing his concern about the long-term impact of such tasks on his career trajectory. He hoped that by setting a clear timeline, he could contribute constructively to the short term without deviating from his career path eventually. This approach aimed to foster a mutual understanding with Amit, ensuring that Mayank's contributions remained aligned with both his and the organization's objectives.

Amit's response was laced with disappointment, reflecting his surprise at Mayank's stance. "Mayank, your reaction is not what I anticipated from someone of your experience and stature within our organization," Amit began, his tone conveying a mix of concern and admonishment. "As a senior member of our team, it's crucial that you exemplify adaptability and commitment, embodying the spirit of teamwork and leadership that we value. Your reluctance to embrace these additional responsibilities sends a concerning message to your team and colleagues."

Amit paused for a moment, letting his words sink in before continuing. "I understand your reservations and your desire to focus on growth-aligned tasks. However, the reality we are facing is a resource constraint that necessitates a collective effort from all of us, regardless of our roles. The essence of leadership is stepping up in challenging times, demonstrating flexibility, and contributing where the organization needs us the most."

He then addressed Mayank's concern about the undefined duration of this arrangement. "I recognize your apprehension about the indefinite nature of these tasks, but I must be candid—there's no fixed timeline for when we'll be able to allocate a dedicated coordinator. Until then, we must all shoulder the responsibilities as they come, ensuring that our collective objectives aren't compromised."

Amit concluded, hoping to bridge the gap between his expectations and Mayank's concerns. "I urge you to reconsider your position, Mayank. Your leadership is not just about steering your direct reports or excelling in your designated role; it is also about being a pillar of strength and resilience for the entire organization. I'm counting on you to reflect on this and understand the broader perspective of what we're trying to achieve here."

Amit's words were meant to underscore the importance of unity and flexibility within the organization, especially during times of scarcity and challenge. He aimed to remind Mayank of the bigger picture and the critical role he plays in not just meeting his individual goals but in contributing to the overarching success of the team and the company.

After meeting Amit, Mayank called Nayan to meet outside the office. Mayank and Nayan took a break together. Mayank looked upset and started talking about his chat with Amit. "Amit wants me to handle more of those coordinator jobs on top of my own work," Mayank said, clearly annoyed. "He thinks I should just accept any work, no matter if it fits my job or not."

Nayan listened and nodded, understanding how tough it was for Mayank. "That's tough. Those extra tasks pull you away from our main goal, which is to help the business grow," Nayan replied, trying to offer some comfort.

Mayank took a deep breath and continued, "Amit told me I should be okay with doing any work because I'm a senior here. He wants me to set a good example. But I don't see how doing a job that's not mine helps anyone."

Nayan leaned back, thinking for a moment. "It's a tricky situation. You want to do what is right for everyone, but not if it stops you from doing your own job well," he said, hoping to help Mayank see things more clearly.

"Yeah," Mayank agreed, looking a bit lost. "Amit said we don't have anyone else to do these tasks and that I should just handle it. It feels like it's not about what I'm good at anymore."

Nayan suggested, "Maybe there's a way to sort this out without it affecting your main work. Could you talk to Amit about finding a better balance?" Mayank thought it over. "I might try, but Amit seems to think that not wanting to do these extra tasks means I'm not being a good leader. It's hard to keep everyone happy while feeling like I'm stuck."

Their break ended, and they both knew they had to go back to work, facing the challenges ahead. This talk did not solve everything, but it helped Mayank feel less alone with his worries.

As time went on, Mayank did his best to juggle the extra responsibilities along with his primary duties. He made sure to keep Amit updated, which seemed to reassure Amit that the work was being handled competently. Mayank's dedication stemmed from his commitment to his role and his desire to meet expectations, even if it meant taking on tasks he was not keen on.

Despite his efforts to perform well in all areas, the stress of managing these additional tasks lingered in the back of his mind. Mayank could not shake off the feeling of being stretched too thin, which was made worse whenever Amit criticized him for any shortcomings. This criticism felt particularly unfair to Mayank, who believed he was going above and beyond his job description. He could not understand why Amit would focus on blaming him instead of offering guidance or recognizing his extra effort.

"Instead of pointing out what's wrong, why can't Amit see how hard I'm trying? I am doing things that are not even part of my job," Mayank thought to himself. This situation left him feeling underappreciated and frustrated, as he felt that his willingness to help was being overlooked in favor of focusing on any mistakes.

That night, Mayank found himself reflecting deeply on his current state of mind. "It looks like my personality is shifting. I have become quicker to anger lately. I dread going to the office now and feel disconnected from my team. This cannot be good; if this continues, it is going to take a toll on my health. It's crucial that I have a serious conversation with Amit and resolve this situation." Mayank realized the importance of addressing his concerns directly with Amit, hoping to find a solution that would allow him to focus on his primary responsibilities without the added stress of tasks he felt were unsuitable for his role.

The next day, Mayank approached Amit and shared his feelings, "Amit, I've spent a lot of time thinking about the tasks I've been assigned. Doing the same repetitive tasks every day, like data entry or copying information, feels pointless. These tasks do not contribute to my growth or learning. They just keep me busy without any real purpose or goals. This type of work will not lead to any recognition for me. I believe we should consider assigning such tasks to others who might benefit more from them. I'd like to focus on the responsibilities outlined in my job description." Mayank hoped this conversation would encourage Amit to reconsider the distribution of tasks, allowing him to focus on work that aligns with his role and professional development goals.

The concept of meaningless work is highly subjective, reflecting individual values, career aspirations, and the quest for purpose and satisfaction in one's career. While Amit found himself without alternative solutions, Mayank had reached a clear conclusion. Given the lack of resolution from their discussion, Mayank ultimately decided that resigning was his best course of action. This decision underscored the importance of aligning one's job with personal and professional goals to ensure a fulfilling career journey.

Key observations from this chapter –

The Importance of Role Clarity: Mayank's frustration stems from being assigned tasks that deviate significantly from his primary responsibilities. This highlights the need for clear role definitions within organizations to ensure employees are engaged in work that leverages their skills and contributes to their professional growth.

Communication is Key: Mayank's decision to have a candid conversation with Amit about the mismatch between his tasks and his role underscores the importance of open communication in the workplace. Employees should feel empowered to express their concerns and aspirations, while managers should be receptive to feedback and willing to explore solutions collaboratively.

Understanding Organizational Needs: Amit's perspective sheds light on the broader organizational context, where flexibility and adaptability are often required from employees, especially in leadership roles. This underscores the need for employees to balance personal career goals with the immediate needs of the organization.

The Impact of Misalignment on Employee Well-being: Mayank's experience illustrates how misalignment between an employee's role and their tasks can lead to frustration, decreased motivation, and even considerations of resignation. This serves as a reminder for organizations to ensure that employees are engaged in meaningful work that aligns with their career goals.

The Value of Meaningful Work: The concept of "meaningless work" varies among individuals but generally refers to tasks that do not utilize an employee's skills, offer growth opportunities, or contribute to their professional satisfaction. Organizations should strive to assign tasks that are perceived as valuable and fulfilling by their employees.

The Role of Leadership: Leadership is not just about assigning tasks but also about recognizing and nurturing the strengths and aspirations of team members. Leaders like Amit should aim to support their employees' professional development and ensure that their responsibilities contribute to their growth.

Career and Personal Growth: Mayank's pursuit of tasks that align with his professional aspirations highlights the importance of seeking opportunities for growth and development. Employees should proactively seek roles and responsibilities that challenge them and offer pathways for advancement.

The Decision to Resign: Mayank's eventual decision to resign is a drastic but sometimes necessary step for individuals who find themselves consistently engaged in work that does not align with their career goals or personal values. It serves as a reminder that employees have the agency to seek environments where they can thrive.

In summary, Mayank's story emphasizes the need for clear communication, role clarity, and the alignment of tasks with individual skills and career aspirations. Both employees and organizations have a role to play in ensuring that work is engaging, meaningful, and conducive to professional growth.

CHAPTER 7

The Ripple Effect

"I'm the first to admit this whole salary thing is getting out of control. In the final analysis, it's still about the work"

– Jim Carrey

Two years had swiftly passed since Anne embarked on a new chapter with a different organization, bringing her total professional experience to over four years. During this time, she had broadened her expertise across various technologies, becoming a versatile and valuable asset to her team. Known for her dedication and cooperative spirit, Anne had seamlessly integrated herself into the fabric of her new workplace, earning the respect and admiration of her colleagues.

Despite her professional accomplishments, Anne's personal life bore the weight of distance. Her family home lay in another city, some 500 miles away from where she currently resided as a paying guest. This separation from her roots often found her nostalgic, especially when it came to the comforts of home. She fondly remembered the delicious meals prepared by her mother, a stark contrast to the food she encountered as a paying guest. The warmth of homemade dishes, imbued with love and familiarity, was something Anne missed deeply. It served as a constant reminder that, no matter the successes and strides made in her career, there truly was no place like home.

Now well-established in her current role, Anne had successfully cultivated a circle of close friends at her workplace, providing her with a much-needed social outlet during the weekends. This network of friends had become an integral part of her life outside of work, offering support, laughter, and companionship, somewhat compensating for the distance from her family.

Professionally, Anne's expertise and understanding of her projects had grown exponentially. She had developed a keen sense of the project requirements, consistently delivering results that not only met but often exceeded expectations. Her dedication and skill had not gone unnoticed; she was recognized as a key performer within her team, admired for her ability to tackle challenges head-on and contribute significantly to the team's success.

A testament to her hard work and team spirit came a few months prior when she was honored with the Best Team Player Award at the company's annual event. This accolade was a significant milestone in her career, symbolizing her commitment to teamwork and her positive impact on those around her. The award was a source of immense pride for Anne, validating her efforts and dedication to her role.

Her reputation for excellence had reached managerial levels, with many knowing her by name due to her outstanding work and active participation on the floor. This recognition within the company underscored her status as a valued employee, whose contributions were crucial to the success of her team and the organization. Anne's journey had evolved from the initial days of missing home comforts to establishing herself as an indispensable member of her workplace, demonstrating the power of hard work, resilience, and the importance of building meaningful connections.

Since the inception of her career, Anne had always been a stellar employee, marked by her diligence and innate talent. Her decision to leave her first job was propelled by the pursuit of better financial prospects, a move that reflected her deep-seated aspiration for personal and family financial growth. However, amidst her career advancements, the absence of familial warmth and the dream of owning a home increasingly weighed on her.

Each day, as Anne made her way from the office to her paying guest accommodation, the sight of towering apartments ignited a longing within her—a longing for a day when she could afford such a residence and invite her parents to live with her. These high-rise buildings stood as silent witnesses to her aspirations, each window echoing her desire for a place to call her own.

Yet, the reality of her situation anchored her dreams firmly to the ground. Financial obligations towards her family back home necessitated that a sizable portion of her earnings be sent to support them. This, coupled with the expenses of her own living costs, left little room for saving towards the dream of purchasing a flat. The dual responsibility of contributing to her family's well-being while managing her expenses meant that her goal of buying a home remained just out of reach, a distant dream that hovered on the horizon of her future.

Over the past two years, Anne had been diligently laying her foundation within the current organization, adapting, learning, and growing in her role. Despite her achievements and the recognition she had garnered, Anne's ambition for greater career advancement remained unquenched. Her recent increment, though a respectable 12% per annum, did not align with her expectations or reflect the value she believed she brought to her team and projects.

Compelled by her conviction and the discrepancy between her contributions and the compensation received, Anne sought a conversation with Ravi, her manager. It was a discussion borne out of not just a desire for fair remuneration but also of Anne's ongoing quest for professional development and recognition. "Ravi, I am not satisfied with what I get as per the work I am doing," she expressed, her voice a blend of determination and the slight frustration of feeling undervalued. This statement was not just about numbers; it reflected Anne's deep commitment to her work and her belief in the importance of an equitable reward for effort and results.

This moment was significant for Anne, marking another instance where she found herself advocating for her worth and career aspirations. It was a testament to her proactive nature and willingness to address issues head-on, characteristics that had propelled her career thus far. Yet, it also underscored the challenges ambitious professionals often face in aligning their perceptions of value with those of their organization. This dialogue with Ravi was not merely a negotiation for better pay but a critical step in Anne's continuous journey to navigate the complexities of career growth, compensation, and personal fulfillment.

Ravi's response was both acknowledging and non-committal. "Anne, there's no doubt you're a valuable member of our team, as evidenced by the award you received. The increment you have been given aligns with the company's assessment of your contributions and work experience. You have been rewarded because you meet, and often exceed, our expectations," Ravi began, his tone conveying appreciation yet bound by the company's policies. "However, I understand your concerns and aspirations. I will discuss this with HR to see if there is any possibility for adjustment. Give me a week, and I'll get back to you with an update."

Despite Ravi's promise to revisit the discussion, Anne's intuition braced her for disappointment. A week later, her anticipation was met with the expected outcome—a negative response regarding any revision to her salary increment. This decision, though anticipated, did not dampen Anne's resolve but rather solidified her determination to seek opportunities that aligned more closely with her aspirations and financial goals.

In the quiet moments following Ravi's update, Anne's thoughts turned towards the future, a future where her ambitions were not tethered by constraints that no longer served her growth. She longed for a lifestyle that mirrored her hard work and achievements, a quality of life that was currently beyond her grasp due to financial limitations. The realization dawned on her that to achieve the lifestyle she envisioned for herself and to support her family as she desired, a significant change was necessary.

Encouraged by the abundance of opportunities in larger cities and equipped with a wealth of experience and a deep understanding of technology, Anne decided to proactively seek new horizons. She became active on job portals and leveraged social media platforms to expand her search. Her profile, rich with experience and marked by a history of excellence, positioned her as a highly attractive candidate in the competitive job market.

This decision to explore opportunities beyond her current organization was driven by more than the pursuit of financial gain; it was about Anne's commitment to personal and professional growth. She recognized that to continue evolving, sometimes a change of environment is essential. As she embarked on this search, Anne was not just looking for a new job; she was seeking a new chapter in her career, one that promised to bring her closer to the dreams she harbored for herself and her loved ones.

Anne's strategic move in her career journey paid off when she secured a new job opportunity that significantly surpassed her current salary, offering her a 40% increase. This leap in financial compensation ignited a spark of hope within her, illuminating a clear path towards achieving her dream of homeownership. The prospect of comfortably managing EMI for a house loan became a tangible reality, bridging the gap between her aspirations and the means to fulfill them.

Despite the comfort and familiarity she found in her current role, Anne was aware that the professional landscape was dynamic, and to truly flourish, one must be open to exploring all possibilities. Armed with the new offer, she saw an opportunity not just for advancement but as a litmus test for her value within her current organization. The decision to approach Ravi about the competing offer was not made lightly; it was a calculated risk, born out of a desire for growth and recognition.

In her mind, Anne rehearsed the conversation, envisioning the different outcomes. She was prepared to navigate the delicate balance between expressing her loyalty to the company and her ambition for personal and professional development. "This discussion with Ravi will be pivotal," she thought. "It's not just about the salary; it's about acknowledging my contributions and the potential for growth here. If Ravi sees the value I bring to the team and is open to matching the offer, it could redefine my career trajectory within this organization."

However, Anne also prepared herself for the possibility of an indifferent response. She understood that the absence of a counteroffer or a genuine attempt to retain her would be a clear indicator that it was time to move on. "If my current employer cannot match or come close to what the new opportunity presents, then submitting my resignation will be the next logical step," she contemplated. "It's a decision not made out of spite but out of respect for my own career and financial goals."

Anne's approach was not one of ultimatum but a genuine attempt to gauge her worth within her current company and explore whether they valued her contributions enough to retain her. This scenario was about more than negotiating salary; it was about seeking recognition and the opportunity to achieve her personal goals without compromising her professional integrity. As she prepared to have this crucial conversation with Ravi, Anne was fueled by a mixture of anticipation and resolve, ready to embrace whatever outcome lay ahead in her journey towards fulfillment and success.

The following morning, as Anne prepared for her day, a decisive moment of clarity swept over her. She found herself contemplating a bold move—one that would unequivocally signal her readiness for a new chapter in her career. The idea of sending her resignation letter before her planned discussion with Ravi emerged not from a place of impulsiveness, but from a strategic thought process aimed at gauging the true value her company placed on her contributions.

Anne understood the gravity of her decision. By submitting her resignation, she was not just leaving her job; she was presenting her employer with a tangible choice: to recognize her worth and make a counteroffer or to let her go. This action would serve as a litmus test, revealing whether her aspirations and contributions were indeed as valued as she hoped.

With this in mind, Anne drafted her resignation letter, imbuing it with a tone of professionalism and gratitude for the opportunities she had been afforded. She carefully articulated her reasons for departure, emphasizing her desire for growth and the pursuit of new challenges.

Upon clicking the send button, a wave of anticipation washed over her. This was a point of no return, a step that could potentially alter the trajectory of her professional life.

Anne's strategy was clear: she would engage in negotiations only if Ravi reached out, expressing a desire to retain her. This would indicate that her contributions were recognized and that the company saw her as an integral part of its future. In sending her resignation, Anne was not severing ties but opening the door for a conversation about her value and future within the organization.

The hours that followed were laden with anticipation. Anne kept a close eye on her inbox and phone, waiting for any sign of Ravi's response although she was aware that response would not come immediately. This period of waiting was not passive; it was a statement of Anne's confidence in her worth and her readiness to embrace new opportunities that aligned with her career goals and financial aspirations.

After three days of silence following her resignation, Anne decided to open up to her close colleagues about her decision. Their reactions were mixed, a blend of surprise and understanding, reflecting the complex emotions that accompany such a significant career move. It wasn't long before Ravi, her manager, requested a personal meeting to discuss her resignation. The anticipation was palpable as Anne prepared to articulate her reasons, not fully aware of how pivotal this conversation could be for her career trajectory.

The meeting room, usually a space for project discussions and strategic planning, transformed into a setting for a deeply personal and potentially career-altering conversation. Anne began with a narrative that touched on her familial obligations, citing her parents' health as a primary reason for her intended departure. This revelation prompted Ravi to explore the depths of Anne's decision, questioning whether her resignation was a final farewell or a plea for flexibility and support from the organization.

Ravi's response to Anne's situation was both surprising and reassuring. He offered a range of accommodation, from extended leave to the possibility of remote work, demonstrating the company's willingness to support its employees through personal challenges. This gesture of understanding and flexibility highlighted the value placed on Anne as a team member and her contributions to the project.

Anne, however, steered the conversation towards a more fundamental issue: her desire to provide a stable and comfortable home for her parents, a goal that extended beyond the immediate concern for their health. This admission shifted the focus from temporary solutions to a more significant, underlying challenge—the financial feasibility of purchasing her own home on her current salary.

Ravi, now understanding the crux of Anne's dilemma, probed further, asking if financial improvement within the organization could influence her decision to stay. Anne's response, a request for a 45 to 50 percent salary increase, set the stage for a more detailed discussion about compensation, expectations, and the reality of the job market. Her benchmark, influenced by the salaries of peers in other companies, painted a picture of the competitive landscape and the pressures it exerts on individual career decisions.

Ravi, confronted with the dual challenge of retaining a valued team member and navigating the company's salary structure, requested additional time to consult with senior management and HR. This request marked a turning point in the conversation, extending a lifeline to Anne's tenure with the company and opening a window for negotiation and compromise.

As Anne agreed to wait for Ravi's response, both parties were left to ponder the implications of their discussion. For Anne, it was a decisive moment, balancing her professional aspirations against personal responsibilities and financial goals. For Ravi, it was a test of his leadership and the organization's ability to adapt to the needs of its employees without setting unsustainable precedents. The days following their meeting were filled with anticipation, as both Anne and Ravi awaited a decision that could redefine Anne's career path and set a precedent for how the company addresses the evolving needs and aspirations of its workforce.

The dilemma surrounding Anne's resignation and subsequent salary negotiation brings to light several key considerations for both management and team dynamics. Ravi's discussion with Anuj, the department head, and the HR representative, sheds light on the complex decision-making process involved in addressing individual employee requests that deviate from the norm.

Anuj's concern about the impact on project margins by increasing Anne's salary by 40% highlights the financial constraints and accountability managers face. Ravi's argument, emphasizing Anne's proven record of accomplishment and the cost-benefit analysis of retaining her versus onboarding a new employee, underscores the value of experienced team members who have demonstrated success in their roles. This consideration is particularly relevant in projects where continuity and client satisfaction are paramount.

The HR representative's caution about setting a precedent resonates with a common dilemma in organizational management: balancing individual contributions and requests with the broader implications for team morale and company policy. Ravi's acknowledgment of this concern, coupled with his focus on business need and client satisfaction, illustrates the delicate balancing act managers must perform between adhering to policies and adapting to specific circumstances.

The decision to process Anne's salary change, although after careful consideration and approval, signifies a willingness to make exceptions for key performers. However, it also raises questions about equity, transparency, and the criteria used to justify such exceptions.

Anne's situation, as she navigates her notice period with an impending offer from another company, exemplifies the challenges employees face when seeking career advancement and financial growth. The resolution of her case, with HR confirming her salary revision just days before her notice period ended, reflects the potential for negotiation and compromise within professional settings.

However, the repercussions of Anne's actions on her colleagues' perceptions highlight an unintended consequence of such negotiations. The speculation among her peers about her motivations—whether it was a strategic move for a salary increase or a genuine need stemming from family circumstances—underscores the importance of communication and transparency in managing career transitions.

This scenario leaves organizations with critical questions to ponder: Is resignation the only level employees feel they must achieve significant salary adjustments? And how can companies proactively address employees' career progression and compensation concerns to prevent such situations?

For organizations, the key takeaway is the necessity of having flexible, yet clear policies on compensation and career development. This includes regular reviews to ensure salaries remain competitive, transparent communication channels for discussing career aspirations, and mechanisms to recognize and reward high performers. Such approaches can help mitigate the need for employees to resort to resignation as a negotiation tactic, fostering a more positive, open, and mutually beneficial work environment.

The scenario with Anne turning down a job offer at the last moment highlights a growing challenge in the recruitment landscape:

candidate reneging. This phenomenon, where candidates back out of accepted job offers, poses significant concerns for recruiters and organizations alike. The implications of such decisions are multifaceted, affecting not just the hiring process but also the strategic planning and operational efficiency of businesses. Here are some insights into the consequences and potential strategies to mitigate this issue:

Consequences for Organizations

Operational Disruption: The sudden withdrawal of a candidate, especially for critical roles, can lead to operational delays. Projects may be put on hold, and the absence of necessary skills can impact productivity and timelines.

Increased Costs: The recruitment process is resource-intensive, involving time, effort, and financial investment. A candidate's last-minute refusal implies that these resources have been expended in vain, necessitating a restart of the recruitment cycle.

Damaged Employer Brand: Frequent occurrences of candidates revoking job offers can tarnish an organization's reputation, making it harder to attract top talent in the future.

Strategic Setbacks: Critical roles are often tied to strategic initiatives. A delay in filling these positions can impede the organization's ability to execute strategic plans, potentially leading to lost opportunities.

Strategies to Mitigate Candidate Reneging

Enhanced Communication: Maintain open and frequent communication with candidates throughout the hiring process. This helps in building a relationship and understanding their concerns and motivations better.

Realistic Job Previews: Providing candidates with a realistic preview of their roles, responsibilities, and the company culture can help in aligning expectations and reducing the chances of last-minute withdrawals.

Engagement Strategies: Engage candidates between the offer acceptance and joining dates through meet-and-greets, company updates, and interactions with future team members. This helps in keeping their interest and commitment levels high.

Signing Bonuses and Conditional Offers: In some cases, offering signing bonuses with conditions attached (such as repayment if the employee leaves within a certain period) can be effective in ensuring candidates' commitment.

Flexibility and Adaptability: Recognize and address any concerns candidates might have regarding relocation, work-life balance, or career progression opportunities. Flexibility in negotiations can sometimes secure a candidate's long-term commitment.

Backup Plans: Always have a backup list of qualified candidates for critical roles. In case of a breakup, this minimizes the time and effort required to restart the recruitment process.

Anne's decision not to join after accepting an offer is a stark reminder of the unpredictable nature of recruitment. While it is impossible to eliminate the risk of candidate reneging entirely, adopting a strategic approach to recruitment, emphasizing communication, engagement, and flexibility, can significantly mitigate its impact. For organizations, adapting to the evolving dynamics of the job market and candidate behavior is crucial in safeguarding their operational and strategic interests.

Key learnings from this chapter for Employees:

Advocacy for Value: Anne's proactive approach to discussing her value and compensation with her manager exemplifies the importance of self-advocacy in the workplace. Employees should feel empowered to communicate their achievements and how they align with their compensation expectations.

Navigating Career Transitions: The decision to seek opportunities elsewhere, driven by a pursuit of better compensation and career growth, highlights the necessity of career mobility in achieving professional goals. Employees should continuously assess their career trajectory and remain open to new opportunities that align with their aspirations.

Strategic Resignations: Anne's calculated risk in submitting her resignation to gauge her employer's willingness to retain her underscores a strategic approach to career negotiations. However, this should be approached with caution, as it can have varying outcomes depending on the employer's response and the employee's market value.

Professional Growth vs. Financial Incentives: The balance between professional development and financial growth is a recurring theme. Employees should weigh their options, considering both the career growth opportunities and the financial benefits of a new role or staying with their current employer.

Key learnings from this chapter for Employers:

Recognizing and Retaining Talent: Anne's story underlines the importance of recognizing and retaining key performers through competitive compensation and acknowledgment of their contributions. Employers should have mechanisms in place to regularly review and adjust compensation to reflect an employee's value to the organization.

Transparent Communication: Ravi's initial non-committal response and later negotiation attempts with Anne illustrate the need for transparent communication regarding compensation policies and potential for growth within the company. Employers should ensure clear channels of communication to manage employee expectations effectively.

Flexibility in Compensation Strategies: The negotiation process between Anne and her manager reveals the need for flexibility in compensation strategies to retain top talent. Employers must balance internal equity with the need to make exceptions for exceptional contributors.

Addressing Counteroffers: The scenario where Anne receives a counteroffer after resigning highlights the complexities of managing counteroffers. Employers should carefully consider the long-term implications of counter offers on team morale and company policy.

Mitigating Recruitment Risks: Anne's last-minute decision to decline a job offer after accepting it points to the risks involved in the recruitment process. Employers should develop strategies to mitigate these risks, such as enhanced candidate engagement and realistic job previews.

Anne's journey through professional growth, negotiation, and decision-making presents a miniature copy of the broader challenges faced by both employees and employers in the contemporary workplace. For employees, it underscores the importance of clear communication, self-advocacy, and strategic career planning. For employers, it emphasizes the need for flexible compensation strategies, recognition of employee value, and effective communication to retain and attract top talent. By understanding and addressing these dynamics, both parties can work towards mutually beneficial outcomes, fostering a productive and satisfying professional environment.

CHAPTER 8

The Professional and Personal Tightrope

"Work life balance is about creating a life that flows with you rather than a life you to power through"

– Jaime Marie Wilson

In today's fast-paced and highly competitive environment, the demand for prompt and efficient service has become a universal expectation. The rapid pace of technological advancements has further fueled this trend, setting a high benchmark for speed and efficiency across various domains. This societal shift is evident in the daily preferences and behaviors of individuals, where patience wears thin at the slightest delay. For instance, it is a common expectation for digital applications to load within a mere 2 to 3 seconds; anything beyond this threshold often results in frustration and a quick shift to alternative solutions. This scenario underscores a broader cultural intolerance for waiting, reflecting a significant increase in anxiety levels and a diminishing capacity for patience in our contemporary lifestyle.

The core objective of any organization, regardless of its industry, is to deliver superior service to its clients. This imperative raises a critical question: What exactly constitutes "better" service? On the surface, it seems to imply that organizations must go to great lengths to satisfy their clients' demands, often pushing the boundaries of speed, quality, and customization. However, this pursuit of client satisfaction brings to the forefront a potential conflict between professional obligations and personal well-being.

The dilemma posited here is profound: Does ensuring client satisfaction necessitate that employees sacrifice their personal time and deprioritize moments spent with their families? This question strikes at the heart of the work-life balance debate, challenging the notion that exceptional client service must come at the cost of personal sacrifices. It prompts a reevaluation of organizational values and practices, advocating for a model that does not implicitly demand that employees forsake their private lives for the sake of professional commitments.

In essence, the quest for superior client service should not overlook the well-being of those tasked with delivering it. Organizations must strive to create a culture that values and respects the importance of work-life balance. This involves implementing policies and practices that allow employees to excel in their roles without compromising their health, happiness, or family time. By doing so, companies can foster a more motivated, satisfied, and productive workforce, which, in turn, enhances the quality of service provided to clients.

The challenge lies in finding a harmonious balance that benefits both the client and the employee. Organizations that succeed in this endeavor are likely to not only achieve higher levels of client satisfaction but also cultivate a loyal and engaged employee base. The ultimate goal should be to redefine what it means to serve clients "better" by ensuring that the pursuit of excellence in client service is aligned with the principles of employee well-being and work-life harmony.

While the notion of work-life balance is often framed in terms of time spent working versus time for personal life, the qualitative aspects of work and personal fulfillment play an equally significant role. Professionals who find joy, purpose, and satisfaction in their work are more likely to remain positive and content, even in the face of demanding work schedules. This underscores the importance of aligning job roles with personal passions, fostering supportive work cultures, and implementing practices that promote flexibility and well-being.

Under Akshat's leadership, the project team faced the challenging task of meeting frequent release milestones, a common scenario in dynamic project environments, especially in software development. Anupama, Anurag, and Rachit, all experienced software engineers with 4 to 5 years under their belts, were juggling the dual responsibilities of enhancing features and addressing existing issues. This dual mandate kept them perpetually busy, a witness to the high-pressure environments prevalent in tech industries.

Anurag's whispered grievance to Anupama, "This is a daily story. We need to deliver everything as mentioned. I cannot even think of managing my personal life. Very irritating," reflects a sentiment common among professionals in high-stakes projects. It captures the essence of the work-life balance struggle, exacerbated by tight deadlines and the expectation of high-quality deliverables.

Anupama smiled and replied "Fully agree that work is too much, and initially I was also thinking in the same way. Then I realized that by getting frustrated, I will get nothing. Rather, it has a negative impact on proper release."

Anupama's response to Anurag brings a perspective shift to the conversation, highlighting a mature approach to handling work stress and the high demands of their project. Her insight touches upon the critical realization that frustration and negativity do not contribute to solutions but rather compound the challenges they face, especially when striving for timely and quality releases. Anupama's realization that frustration only serves to hinder progress emphasizes the importance of maintaining a constructive mindset, even in the face of overwhelming demands. Her approach suggests a focus on aspects of work that individuals can control, such as their reactions to stress, time management, and the quality of their output. This proactive stance can help mitigate feelings of helplessness and improve overall productivity. Most importantly, Anupama's attitude reflects an understanding that resilience—bouncing back from setbacks and maintaining focus on objectives—is key to both personal well-being and professional success.

Anurag, with a tone that mixed resignation with determination, continued to articulate his stance, emphasizing the nuanced balance he sought between his professional commitments and personal life. "I fully acknowledge our collective responsibility towards ensuring a successful and timely release," he began, his words reflecting a deep understanding of the expectations resting on their shoulders. "However," he added, pausing for a moment to choose his words carefully, "the fulfillment of this duty shouldn't come at the expense of my personal time. Sacrificing the moments that are meant for rest, for family, or for pursuing personal interests, is a price too steep for me."

His voice grew firmer as he addressed the issue of extended work hours, a practice increasingly becoming the norm in their line of work. "I've always believed that efficiency and productivity are not about how many hours we're glued to our desks, but about how effectively we use our working hours. The idea of routinely working late into the night or dedicating weekends to work is something I find fundamentally misaligned with my principles."

Anurag's perspective was not just about personal preference; it was a stand on the broader issue of work-life balance. "The essence of our lives outside work can't be underestimated — it's where we find joy, connection, and rejuvenation. These aspects are crucial not just for our personal well-being but for sustaining our creativity and productivity at work. Continuously encroaching on this personal time, in my view, diminishes our work's quality and our quality of life."

In his reflection, Anurag encapsulated a growing sentiment among professionals today — the need for a work environment that respects individual boundaries and values the holistic well-being of its employees. His words called for a shift in perspective, urging a reevaluation of how success is measured and achieved, advocating for a culture where personal time is not sacrificed at the altar of professional responsibilities. Anupama shifted her focus towards Anurag, signaling a pause in her own work to address the conversation with the seriousness it warranted. "Anurag, let's consider for a moment the origin of these deadlines. Do you genuinely believe that Akshat unilaterally imposes these timelines on us? From my perspective, it seems we collectively agree upon these delivery dates after thorough discussion, which in turn informs Akshat's commitments to our clients," she reasoned, attempting to shed light on the collaborative nature of their project timelines.

Anurag, not entirely swayed, countered with a reminder of their shared humanity and the inherent unpredictability it brings. "Yes, I understand the process of setting these timelines, but we're human. Delays can happen, and sometimes they are beyond our control," he argued, emphasizing the need for flexibility, and understanding in their workflow.

Recognizing the complexity of the discussion and the need to prioritize immediate work tasks, Anupama proposed a pause in their conversation. "We should delve deeper into this tomorrow," she suggested, indicating the importance of the discussion but also acknowledging the immediate need to maintain project momentum. "Right now, I need to provide some tasks to Rachit to ensure his work isn't impacted."

With that, Anupama redirected her attention back to her laptop, resuming her work with a renewed focus. Her actions underscored a pragmatic approach to workplace challenges, balancing the need for ongoing dialogue about work-life balance and project commitments with the immediate demands of their roles and responsibilities.

On Friday, Akshat knew everyone was ready for the weekend, but they had a big project update due on Monday. He gathered his team to check if everything was on track.

He asked, "Have you all finished your work and checked everything?" hoping for good news.

Rachit hesitated before saying, "There's a bit of a problem. I'm behind because I was waiting on some things from Anupama, so I haven't finished testing everything yet."

Akshat was worried. "So, we can't finish by Monday without the testing done?" he asked, knowing how important the deadline was.

Rachit promised, "Don't worry, I said we'd be done by Monday, and I'll make sure of it. I'll work over the weekend to finish up."

Anurag watched this exchange and felt frustrated. He thought, "It's because of people like Rachit, always promising to work extra, that the rest of us look bad if we don't do the same. They get praised, and we look like we're not team players."

This situation showed the tricky balance between getting work done and keeping a healthy personal life, and how different people handle it in a team. In the midst of their discussion, Akshat shifted his focus towards Anurag, eager to get an update on his portion of the project. With a direct approach, he questioned, "Anurag, can you share where you stand with your tasks?"

Anurag, with a hint of concern in his voice, admitted, "I've encountered a snag that's proving to be quite complex. It's going to require additional time to resolve." Akshat, surveying the room, addressed the group with a sense of urgency, "I understand the challenges, but we must remember our commitment. The release is scheduled for Monday, and we must meet that deadline. Anurag, what is your plan for overcoming this obstacle by tomorrow?"

Anurag's response was unexpected, "Akshat, I'm afraid I won't be available this weekend. We have plans to visit our hometown, and it won't be feasible for me to work from there."

This exchange not only highlighted the pressures of meeting project deadlines but also underscored the personal commitments and challenges faced by team members, adding another layer of complexity to the project's timely completion.

Akshat's tone was tinged with frustration as he addressed Anurag, "And how do you propose we maintain our commitment as a team if you're unavailable?" His question was pointed, reflecting the weight of the situation.

Without hesitation, Anurag offered a solution, albeit a simplistic one, "Why not inform them that the release will be on Tuesday instead?"

Akshat, visibly taken aback, responded with a mix of disbelief and concern, "You all were the ones who agreed upon these timelines, and based on that, I've made promises to our client. They have organized their schedule around our delivery for further demonstrations. Now, Anurag, are you suggesting that we ask our client to rearrange their entire agenda because of personal commitments? This can't be a serious suggestion."

Anurag's frustration was tangible as he countered, "But we have personal lives. How is it fair to expect us to work through every weekend?"

Akshat responded firmly, emphasizing accountability, "The question is, who is behind on their deadlines? You are. If this is the result of your delays, should Anupama and Rachit also sacrifice their weekends because of that? If you cannot meet your commitments, is it fair to drag them into this as well? I expect this task to be completed by tomorrow. I'm sorry, but your personal plans cannot take precedence in this scenario."

The air was thick with tension as Anurag, seething with anger, remained silent. Though he said nothing, his expression conveyed a deep sense of injustice, feeling as if employees were seen merely as tools to be used relentlessly. After Akshat exited the room, Anurag followed, visibly upset. However, Rachit interjected, asking him to stay a moment longer. Anupama, having her own tasks to attend to, left them to their discussion.

Rachit, noticing how upset Anurag was, tried to smooth things over. "Look, Anurag, I get why you're mad. I did not mean to make it seem like we should always work weekends. I was just trying to fix a big problem quickly, not make things worse for us. I did not want to mess up our work-life balance, honestly. I was just thinking about the project, not about making more work for everyone," Rachit said, hoping to calm Anurag down and show him that he was not trying to make their lives harder.

Rachit, sensing Anurag's frustration, tried to offer some comfort. "I understand how you feel about our work taking over our personal lives. I have been there too," Rachit said. "I'm here for you, and I'll help you out tomorrow so we can sort everything out quickly. That way, you will not miss your personal commitments. Also, I've got a story from my previous job that might change the way you see work-life balance."

Anurag, still upset but grateful for Rachit's offer, was curious. "Thanks for stepping up to help, Rachit. I appreciate it. So, what is this story you want to share?" Rachit was ready to share his experience, hoping it might give Anurag a new perspective on balancing work and life, showing him that while the struggle is real, solutions and support within the team can make a significant difference.

Rachit continued, seeking to connect with Anurag's own experiences, "In that role, the expectation was clear, but the reality often stretched beyond those hours. It was about ensuring that critical services were always up and running, no matter what. And yes, there were nights when I had to dive into work unexpectedly, disrupting my personal plans."

Anurag listened intently, relating to Rachit's words, and imagining the pressure of having to be on-call, ready to tackle emergencies at any moment. "So, you're saying you had to be ready to work outside of those agreed hours if something urgent came up?" Anurag asked, trying to grasp the full extent of Rachit's commitment to his role.

"Yes, exactly," Rachit affirmed. "But what made it manageable was the understanding and support from the manager and the clear communication with the client about what constitutes a real emergency.

It wasn't about sacrificing all my personal time; it was about finding a balance and ensuring that when I was needed, I could make a real difference."

Anurag nodded, beginning to see the complexity of balancing urgent work demands with personal life, and how mutual support could alleviate some of the burden. Rachit's story was shedding light on the nuanced reality of work-life balance, beyond the frustration of extended hours.

Rachit's story brought a new perspective to Anurag, highlighting the challenges of managing work expectations and the importance of clear communication and boundaries. Rachit's experience in his previous company, where he was overwhelmed by constant demands without adequate support, served as a cautionary tale. It underscored the necessity for teams and clients to understand the limitations of what can be realistically accomplished without sacrificing the well-being of employees.

Anurag, reflecting on Rachit's words, began to see his situation with Akshat in a different light. The comparison made him realize that while feeling pressured, his scenario was not as dire as Rachit's had been. Akshat's expectations for the project's completion were based on commitments made by the team, including Anurag himself.

The conversation with Rachit was a turning point for Anurag. He recognized the importance of meeting his responsibilities and how his actions impacted not just his own workload but also the team's dynamics and the company's commitments to clients. This realization helped him to see the value in prioritizing his tasks, managing his time more effectively, and communicating more openly about any challenges he faced.

Grateful for Rachit's insights and support, Anurag felt a renewed sense of purpose and commitment to his work. The dialogue between them not only cleared the air but also strengthened their professional relationship, fostering a more collaborative and understanding team environment. This experience was a valuable lesson for Anurag in balancing his professional obligations with his personal life, ultimately leading to more fulfilling and productive work experience.

The story highlights several important observations about work-life balance, team dynamics, and the management of professional responsibilities:

Communication and Collaboration: Effective communication within a team is crucial. Acknowledging the collective responsibility for meeting deadlines allows for a more cooperative approach to problem-solving and workload management. Anupama's and Rachit's interactions with Anurag demonstrate the importance of discussing concerns and finding mutual support to address work challenges.

Setting Realistic Expectations: It is essential for teams to set realistic deadlines and expectations, considering the human aspect of work. Anurag's pushback against working over the weekend underlines the need for balancing professional commitments with personal life, suggesting that project timelines should be realistic and considerate of personal boundaries.

Leadership and Understanding: Akshat's leadership style, focusing on meeting client commitments at the cost of personal time, brings to light the role of managers in fostering a healthy work-life balance. Leaders should strive to understand their team's capacities and limitations, working together to find solutions that do not overly sacrifice personal time.

Prioritizing Employee Well-being: The narrative underscores the importance of prioritizing employee well-being alongside client satisfaction. Organizations should implement policies and practices that support work-life balance, recognizing that the well-being of employees directly impacts productivity and job satisfaction.

Mutual Support and Flexibility: Rachit's offer to help Anurag, despite the pressure to meet deadlines, illustrates the value of mutual support within teams. Flexibility and willingness to assist each other can alleviate individual stress and contribute to the team's overall success.

Personal Responsibility and Reflection: Anurag's realization, prompted by Rachit's story, about the importance of fulfilling professional responsibilities without excuses, highlights personal accountability. Reflecting on one's role and contributions to the team's goals can lead to personal growth and better management of work-life balance.

Learning from Experiences: Rachit's recounting of his previous job experience serves as a learning opportunity for Anurag, showing that challenges related to work-life balance and emergency responses are common in many workplaces. Learning from such experiences can guide individuals in navigating similar situations more effectively in the future.

The story reflects the complexities of balancing professional obligations with personal life in a high-pressure work environment. It advocates for a collective effort from both employees and management to communicate openly, set realistic expectations, and support each other. A culture that values and promotes work-life balance can lead to more satisfied employees, better teamwork, and improved performance.

CHAPTER 9

The Quest for Integrity

"Pleasure in the job puts perfection in the work."

– Aristotle

Aditya stepped into his new role as a Training Manager with a blend of excitement and anticipation. His move to a new organization was a significant leap in his career, and amidst this transition, a childhood story echoed in his mind, offering both a reflection and a contrast to his current sentiments.

The story was about a farmer who, seeking a fresh start, decided to migrate to another village. On the outskirts of his new home, there lived a saint, renowned for his deep devotion and selfless service to the villagers. The farmer, curious and somewhat cautious about the unfamiliar community he was about to join, thought it wise to seek the saint's counsel. He hoped to collect insight into the nature of the people he would soon call his neighbors.

Approaching the saint, the farmer inquired, "What kind of people live in this village?" The saint, peering into the farmer's soul with a gentle gaze, replied with a question of his own, "What kind of people were there in your village?"

The farmer didn't hesitate, his response laced with bitterness, "They were jealous, angry, dishonest, and non-cooperative." Without missing a beat, the saint offered a quiet yet profound response, "Here, you will find the same kind of people."

As Aditya recalled this tale, a smile played on his lips. The story's moral, suggesting that our perceptions about others often shape our reality. He found himself in the shoes of the farmer, on the brink of integrating into an unfamiliar environment, pondering on the wisdom imparted by the saint.

However, unlike the farmer, Aditya's internal dialogue revealed a divergence in belief. The story championed the idea that our external experiences are heavily influenced by our internal attitudes and expectations. Yet, Aditya wrestled with this notion. Despite understanding the moral—that one's perspective can significantly color their encounters with others—he could not fully subscribe to the belief that his perceptions alone dictate the entirety of his experiences.

This introspection led Aditya to a broader survey about human interactions and the complexity of relationships. He acknowledged that while perceptions do play a crucial role in shaping our experiences, the reality of human nature and community dynamics is multifaceted. It involves many factors beyond individual attitudes, including cultural norms, social structures, and the inherent diversity of human character.

Aditya's reflection on the story, thus, was not just a moment of nostalgia but a profound engagement with the narrative's deeper implications. Aditya, upon joining his new role as a Training Manager, could not help but draw parallels between the workplace dynamics he encountered and the fictional tale of the farmer's village from his childhood. He found a striking resemblance in the underlying ethos of his new organization to that of his previous one, much like the farmer's experience of finding similar dispositions in a different village. Aditya observed that the predominant culture across various departments—from HR to Sales, to Procurement—was not necessarily about advancing through merit or adhering to proper procedures. Instead, the unspoken goal was currying favor with superiors. It became evident to him that securing the bosses' approval was the key to unlocking support and resources within the company, an aspect he found dishearteningly universal.

Aditya was well aware that where there are human interactions and gossiping, office politics are almost inevitable. However, he had always prided himself on being the kind of individual who prioritizes substance over superficiality, focusing on his work rather than partaking in idle gossip. He noticed an unsettling trend in the organization: a prevalent lack of open communication. The environment was such that employees felt compelled to censor their thoughts, fearing misinterpretation or misuse of their words. This, to Aditya, was a classic hallmark of a politically charged workplace.

Reflecting on his experiences in previous roles, Aditya recalled moments when he had to seek assistance from senior colleagues, an act that felt more like petition than collaboration. He questioned whether such dynamics truly fostered team spirit.

This self-introspection led him to a critical realization about the nature of personal and professional interactions. Aditya understood that while he might strive to remain authentic and dedicated to his work, the broader organizational culture and its politics could influence how his actions and intentions were perceived. He faced the challenge of maintaining his integrity and work ethic in an environment that valued allegiance to hierarchy over genuine talent and effort. Through this journey, Aditya sought to find a balance between adapting to the prevailing culture and staying true to his principles, all while considering the profound ways in which his presence and personality might affect the fabric of his new workplace.

Amidst the undercurrents of unspoken fears and the stifling lack of freedom to express oneself, Aditya reached a pivotal decision—to leave his current position. The decisive factor propelling his resignation was the prevalent company culture, characterized by personalized policies that catered to the fancies of those in power. In this environment, success and recognition were not necessarily the fruits of hard work and dedication but rather the result of soothing the influential figures within the organization.

To Aditya, it became clear that this was a realm making the right connections and keeping these influencers satisfied could lead to rewards, promotions, and substantial salary increases. Conversely, failure to align oneself with these unwritten rules of engagement could result in being marginalized or even ousted from the company.

This realization was disheartening for someone who valued integrity, fairness, and a merit-based system. Aditya saw such practices as symbolic of a negative work culture—one that prioritized personal allegiances over professional merit and collective achievement. The implications of such a culture were far-reaching, affecting not just individual careers but also the overall morale and productivity of the organization.

Faced with the prospect of compromising his values or struggling in an environment antithetical to his principles, Aditya chose to seek opportunities elsewhere. His decision was rooted in a deep-seated belief that a healthy, positive work culture is essential for personal growth, job satisfaction, and the fostering of genuine team spirit. He aspired to find a workplace that embraced transparency, encouraged open dialogue, and rewarded individuals based on their contributions and abilities, rather than their ability to navigate office politics.

In many organizations, the notice period is seen merely as a procedural step towards an employee's departure. However, in some cases, the corporate culture can dramatically shift, treating outgoing employees as challengers rather than valued team members transitioning to new opportunities. This shift is often marked by senior management perceiving the departing employee's actions with suspicion, dubbing them as contrary to the organization's interests. Increased scrutiny of their work has become commonplace.

Aditya experienced this harsh reality firsthand. Having dedicated six years of his life to his organization, the moment he submitted his resignation, the treatment he received took a stark turn. The recognition for his contributions evaporated; he was abruptly excluded from award considerations for his achievements and was removed from the increments cycle. Despite having no ongoing dependencies that required his presence, his requests for leave were denied. Furthermore, the management went as far as to withhold his variable pay, a move that underscored their punitive stance towards his decision to leave.

The transition was jarring for Aditya. The organization that had been his professional home for six years suddenly regarded him as a foe, simply because he chose to pursue a different path for his career. This treatment left him feeling marginalized and betrayed, questioning the value of his loyalty and hard work over the years. It highlighted a troubling aspect of corporate culture where employees are valued only as long as they remain within the fold, and their departure triggers a response that can feel both personal and vindictive.

Aditya's story underscores the need for organizations to reassess how they handle departures. Rather than viewing them as a loss or betrayal, it is crucial to recognize them as a natural part of the career lifecycle. Adopting a more supportive and respectful approach to notice periods can not only preserve professional relationships but also bolster the company's reputation as a fair and considerate employer.

Aditya's journey from contemplating a childhood story about perceptions shaping realities to navigating the complexities of workplace dynamics and culture in his role as a Training Manager offers several key observations:

Perception Shapes Reality: Aditya's reflection on the childhood story highlights the profound impact of our perceptions on our experiences. This principle is not only applicable in personal interactions but also plays a crucial role in professional environments. How we perceive our colleagues, work culture, and organizational ethos can significantly influence our engagement, satisfaction, and performance at work.

Workplace Culture and Dynamics: Aditya's experiences underscore the importance of workplace culture and the underlying dynamics that govern interactions within an organization. A culture that prioritizes favoritism over meritocracy, as Aditya observed, can choke creativity, innovation, and fairness, leading to disillusionment among employees who value integrity and hard work.

Navigating Office Politics: The necessity to navigate office politics, even for those who prefer to focus solely on their work, is a reality in many organizations.

The Importance of Open Communication: Aditya's observation of the lack of open communication within his organization points to a critical aspect of a healthy work culture. Environments where employees fear expressing their views can lead to a lack of innovation, suppressed dissent, and ultimately, a disengaged workforce.

Impact of Leadership and Policies: The narrative illustrates how personalized policies and leadership styles that cater to the whims of power holders can create a toxic work environment. Leadership that rewards fawning over talent and effort can demoralize employees, leading to a culture of compliance rather than one of collaboration and growth.

Handling Departures with Dignity: Aditya's treatment during his notice period serves as a cautionary tale for organizations. How a company manages departures can significantly affect its reputation, employee morale, and the departing employee's perception of the organization. A respectful and supportive approach to transitions can enhance the company's image as a fair and considerate employer.

Personal Integrity vs. Organizational Culture: Aditya's decision to leave the organization reflects the difficult choice many professionals face when their values do not align with their workplace's culture. It underscores the importance of finding an environment that not only recognizes but also rewards integrity, fairness, and merit.

The Search for a Positive Work Environment: Ultimately, Aditya's story is a quest for a positive and healthy work culture that fosters growth, rewards merit, and encourages open dialogue. It serves as a reminder of the crucial role that organizational culture plays in job satisfaction, employee retention, and overall company success.

Aditya's narrative is a powerful reflection on the complexities of workplace culture and the impact of personal and organizational values on professional life. It serves as a reminder of the importance of aligning personal values with those of the workplace and the ongoing challenge of navigating office politics while maintaining personal integrity.

CHAPTER 10

Beyond the Notice Period

"Doubt kills more dreams than failure ever will".

– Suzy Kassem

In delving into the experiences of Anne, Mayank and many others, readers are invited into a world that mirrors their own professional landscapes, striking a chord with the universal truths of modern employment. These stories are not mere narratives but reflections of the shared journey many of us undertake in our careers. In today's dynamic job market, the concept of lifelong employment at a single organization seems increasingly like a relic of the past. The workforce is characterized by fluidity, with professionals navigating through various roles and organizations in pursuit of fulfillment and growth.

This book does not advocate for resignation as the only path forward. Instead, it seeks to light the numerous reasons that lead individuals to contemplate such a significant step. It explores the intricate dance between personal aspirations and professional realities, and how sometimes, the pursuit of a more aligned and satisfying career trajectory necessitates a change. It delves into the tough decisions employees face when the fabric of their current roles no longer supports their growth or well-being.

Through the lens of Anne, Mayank, and others, the narrative examines the complexities of the notice period—a threshold that is not merely about leaving but about what lies beyond. It reveals the multifaceted negotiations that often occur, from grappling with counter offers to wrestling with the moral and emotional implications of departure. These decisions are not made lightly but are the culmination of deep reflection on one's values, career goals, and the search for a work environment that resonates with one's personal and professional identity.

Furthermore, the book casts a light on the reality that, at times, employees find themselves at a crossroads, having to choose between compromise and the courage to seek new horizons. It acknowledges the resilience and introspection required to make such choices, whether they involve staying and embracing the situation, negotiating for better terms, or ultimately deciding to embark on new ventures.

In essence, this narrative is a mirror to the evolving landscape of work, where the journey through different organizations becomes a testament to an individual's quest for a career that not only challenges and rewards but also aligns with their evolving personal and professional ethos. It is a celebration of the courage to seek fulfillment and the wisdom to recognize when change is necessary, offering insights into the delicate balance of navigating one's career in the ever-changing world of work.

On the internet, there are many surveys on why people leave any organization. In one of the surveys from April '21 to April '22, most common reasons for quitting the job are –

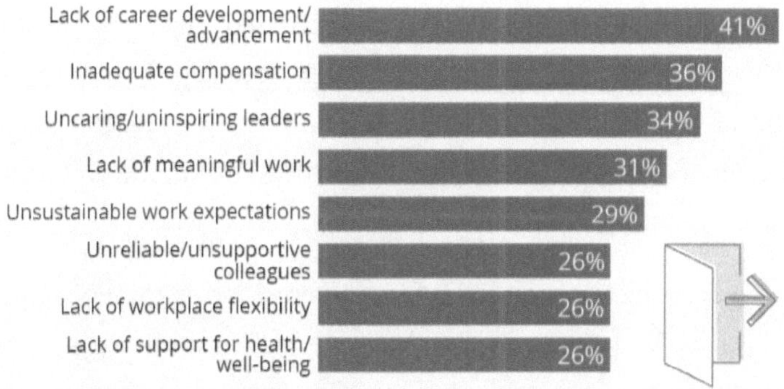

This survey was based on more than 13,000 employees in Australia, Canada, India, Singapore, US and United Kingdom (source McKinsey & Company)

According to Great Place to Work & O.C. Tanner's below information is equally important for the leadership team to understand and work for employees. According to them, 37% of people need to be recognized in an organization. There are 24% employees who want to inspire them and give more autonomy to them. Other areas include more salary, promotion, training, and others.

According to Gallup Workplace Consulting and Global Research, recognition to employees matters a most if received from –

- Manager – 28%
- Company Leader – 24%
- Manager's manager – 12%
- Customer – 10%
- Peer – 9%
- Other – 17%

Upon transitioning to a new organization, Siddharth initially felt a sense of accomplishment and excitement, lifted by the significant salary increase that had prompted his move. However, as the months unfolded in his new role, a sense of nostalgia and longing began to take root within him. Siddharth found himself recalling the rich tapestry of relationships he had woven at his previous workplace—ties that had extended beyond the confines of professional duties and into the realm of genuine friendship.

His former colleagues, ranging from seniors and managers to peers, had become an integral part of his daily life, contributing to a work environment that was not just about achieving targets but also about shared experiences, laughter, and mutual support. These relationships had provided a unique flavor to his work life, infusing his days with a sense of camaraderie, and belonging that he now realized was conspicuously absent in his current setting.

The realization dawned on Siddharth that while the allure of a higher salary was undeniable, the intangible aspects of a job—such as the culture of the workplace, the quality of interpersonal relationships, and the sense of community—played a crucial role in overall job satisfaction. The friendships he had formed with his seniors, managers, and peers had offered him not just professional guidance but also emotional support, making challenging days more manageable and successes more enjoyable.

This reflection led Siddharth to understand that the decision to change jobs, while often driven by financial considerations, involves a complex interplay of factors that affect one's happiness and fulfillment at work. The bonds forged in a workplace contribute significantly to an individual's sense of well-being, and their absence can leave a void that salary increments alone cannot fill.

As Siddharth navigated his new role, he began to appreciate more fully the value of workplace relationships in enriching one's professional journey. This insight encouraged him to actively seek out and cultivate similar bonds in his new organization, recognizing that while the structure and culture of different workplaces may vary, the human desire for connection and camaraderie remains a constant. Through this process of adaptation and growth, Siddharth embarked on a quest to recreate the sense of community he had cherished, understanding now that the essence of a rewarding career encompasses both the tangible benefits and the intangible joys derived from meaningful relationships at work.

Siddharth's journey in his new organization brought him face to face with a crucial realization: the absence of meaningful connections and companionship among colleagues could transform even the most lucrative job into a challenging ordeal. The stark environment, where interactions were strictly professional and the warmth of personal connections was missing, underscored for him the importance of a supportive and engaging workplace community. He understood that the main reason for being part of an organization is to perform work-related duties, but a truly satisfying job experience goes beyond just completing tasks and achieving goals. The real value and fulfillment in a job comes from the emotional connections and the support that team members provide for each other. In other words, a fulfilling job is not just about what you do, but also about the relationships you build and the collaborative environment you are part of, where there is a shared effort and mutual assistance among colleagues.

Confronted with this realization, Siddharth found himself at a junction. The void of interpersonal relationships in his current role frankly contrasted with the vibrant, supportive atmosphere he had left behind. The thought of continuing in an environment devoid of emotional connections weighed heavily on him, highlighting the importance of a workplace that values and fosters personal interactions alongside professional achievements.

In a move driven by both nostalgia and a deep understanding of what he valued most in his professional life, Siddharth reached out to his former manager. He expressed a genuine desire to return to the environment where he felt more than just an employee fulfilling tasks—a place where he felt part of a community. Unexpectedly, an opportunity had opened that matched Siddharth's skills and experience. His previous contributions and exceptional performance had left a lasting impression, making his desire to return a welcomed proposition.

Siddharth's reintegration into his former workplace was marked by a sense of coming home. The familiar faces, the shared history, and the bonds of friendship that had persisted even in his absence welcomed him back with open arms. This reunion underscored a profound lesson about the nature of work and the critical role that interpersonal relationships play in shaping our professional experiences.

His decision to return was not just a step back to a previous job but a stride towards a career path enriched by meaningful connections and shared values. Siddharth's journey illuminated the nuanced balance between professional growth and personal happiness, emphasizing that true success is found not only in achievements and accolades but in the joy and fulfillment derived from being part of a supportive and connected community.

Same happened with Srishti. Her transition to a new job brought with it the promise of fresh opportunities and the anticipation of a supportive work environment, especially concerning her need to balance professional responsibilities with caring for her daughter. However, as time passed, the reality of her new workplace began to diverge from her expectations. The initial assurances of flexibility and support gradually faded, replaced by the rigid demands of her role that left little room for the personal adjustments she had previously enjoyed. This shift not only impacted her work performance but also strained her ability to provide the care and attention her daughter required.

The glaring contrast between her current situation and the supportive atmosphere of her former organization became increasingly apparent. In her previous role, Srishti had experienced a level of understanding and accommodation from her manager and HR that went beyond mere professional courtesy. It was a genuine support system that recognized the importance of work-life balance and the unique challenges faced by working parents. This environment had allowed her to thrive professionally while ensuring her daughter received the care and attention she needed.

Faced with the growing realization that her current job could not offer the same level of support, Srishti began to contemplate a return to her former workplace. The thought of going back was bolstered by the parting words from her previous employer, who had extended an open invitation to return should she ever wish to. This gesture of goodwill now appeared as a beacon of hope, a potential path back to a work environment that valued and supported its employees' personal lives as much as their professional achievements.

With a mixture of hope and apprehension, Srishti reached out to her former manager, expressing her desire to return and the circumstances that prompted her departure. To her relief and joy, her request was met with understanding and empathy. The organization welcomed her back, recognizing the value she brought to the team and the importance of providing a supportive environment for its employees.

Srishti's return to her previous job was more than just a career move; it was a reaffirmation of the importance of a workplace culture that respects and accommodates the personal needs of its employees. Her experience underscores the significance of an empathetic and flexible work environment, especially for employees juggling professional responsibilities with personal commitments. Srishti's story serves as a powerful reminder that while career opportunities can be enticing, the true measure of a job's worth often lies in the support and understanding it offers to its employees, allowing them to excel both in their careers and their personal lives.

The decision to return to a previous employer is a testament to the profound impact that an organization's culture, its people, and its policies can have on an individual. It's not merely the brand or an achievement of the company that draws former employees back, but rather the deep connections formed with colleagues, the alignment with the company's values, and the sense of belonging within its culture. These elements combined create an environment where individuals feel valued, supported, and understood, transcending the conventional employer-employee relationship to something much more meaningful.

Entry and exit from an organization are inevitable phases in one's professional life, yet they are moments laden with potential for lasting impressions. The way a company facilitates these transitions can significantly influence how former employees reflect on their time there and whether they might consider rejoining in the future. An organization that treats these moments with respect, understanding, and appreciation not only leaves a positive mark on the individual's journey but also strengthens its reputation as a desirable place to work.

The essence of this dynamic is beautifully encapsulated in the notion that every action leaves a mark on our journey. It underscores the importance of every interaction, every policy enacted, and every cultural nuance in shaping an individual's experience and perception of the workplace. How others will remember these interactions is crucial—it speaks volumes about the organization's character and can become a powerful factor in attracting or repelling talent.

The legacy of an organization in the hearts and minds of its past employees is built on the quality of the connections it fosters, the inclusivity of its culture, and the fairness of its policies. These are the attributes that individuals carry with them long after they have moved on, and they are the reasons some may choose to return. Thus, an organization's true credibility is measured not by its market success alone but by the enduring impact it has on the lives of those who have been part of its story, however briefly.

The stories mentioned in previous chapters in this book present a vivid tableau of the contemporary work environment, offering a reflective lens on the complexities of modern employment landscapes. These narratives are not just tales; they are echoes of the collective experience, resonating with the familiar challenges and decisions that shape our professional journeys.

In an era where the notion of lifelong tenure at a single organization fades into obsolescence, the workforce is characterized by its dynamic nature. Professionals are increasingly navigating a tangle of opportunities, seeking roles and environments that not only promise growth and fulfillment but also align with their evolving aspirations and values. This fluidity in career paths underscores a broader trend towards seeking satisfaction and alignment in one's professional life, beyond the confines of traditional employment models.

The content delves into the nuanced realities of contemplating resignation, a decision often fraught with a mix of personal and professional considerations. It highlights the intricate balance between the pursuit of career advancement and the quest for a work environment that nurtures one's well-being and professional ethos. Through the experiences shared, the narrative sheds light on the numerous reasons that compel individuals to consider such a pivotal step—from seeking better alignment with personal values to the desire for growth opportunities that their current roles may not provide.

Moreover, the exploration of the notice period reveals the complexity of this transitional phase. It is depicted not just as a procedural step, but as a period of introspection, negotiation, and sometimes, reconciliation with the impending change. The narrative acknowledges the emotional and moral dilemmas that often accompany the decision to leave, as well as the potential for renegotiation and reevaluation of one's place within an organization.

The content underscores the resilience required to navigate these career crossroads, whether one chooses to stay, negotiate for better terms, or venture into new opportunities. It celebrates the courage to pursue a fulfilling career and the wisdom to recognize when change is essential, offering insights into the delicate art of managing one's career amidst the ever-evolving landscape of work.

Additionally, the content references surveys and research from reputable sources, providing empirical evidence to the reasons behind job changes and the importance of recognition and support within the workplace. These findings underscore the significance of feeling valued and supported in one's role, highlighting the impact of managerial recognition and the need for autonomy and inspiration in fostering a satisfying work environment.

The stories of Siddharth and Srishti further enrich the narrative, illustrating the emotional and practical dimensions of transitioning between jobs. Their experiences emphasize the importance of workplace culture, interpersonal relationships, and support systems in contributing to job satisfaction and personal well-being. Their journeys back to former employers underscore the value of nurturing positive workplace environments where employees feel valued, supported, and connected.

In conclusion, this book's content offers a panoramic view of the modern professional's journey, emphasizing the importance of aligning one's work with personal and professional values. It serves as a reminder of the dynamic nature of careers today and the ongoing quest for fulfillment in the workplace. Through the stories shared, readers are encouraged to reflect on their own paths, armed with the insight that every step taken is a part of a larger journey towards finding or creating work environments that resonate with their deepest aspirations and values.